FOREWORD

I first encountered *The Seafarers* several years ago, as a reference in Julian Smith's biography of Nevil Shute. I also learned in the biography that Nevil Shute's surviving papers, the originals of which are kept in the Australian National Library in Canberra, had been microfilmed and archived at Syracuse University in New York.

I obtained copies of all his unpublished manuscripts from Syracuse University, read them, and, shared them with other Shutists around the world. There were two versions of *The Seafarers* in the unpublished manuscripts, both of which at first seemed to be only approximations of *Blind Understanding,* which in turn was a predecessor to *Requiem for a Wren.* The three unpublished manuscripts, and the one published novel, were all studies of the effects of post-war peace on the people who dedicated their youths to the defense of England and the defeat of Germany.

Nevil Shute wrote the first draft of *The Seafarers* sometime around 1946–47. He thought enough of his first effort to rewrite the entire manuscript shortly thereafter. However, he apparently did not think either was worthy of publication. In 1948, he rewrote the story as *Blind Understanding,* another tale of the after-effects of war. In it, he included many of the scenes and topics later to be found in *Requiem for a Wren.* He must have been dissatisfied with that version as well, as he put it aside. *Requiem for a Wren* was the only one of this developmental sequence to be published. While the relationship of these stories is obvious, it was not at first so obvious that they constitute entirely different plots, with different characters, and different outcomes.

After a bit of prodding from other Shutists to whom I had loaned copies of the manuscripts, I began to realize that *The Seafarers* was not just an approximation of another book; it was a fine story in itself. Added to this, Fred Weiss, owner of The Paper Tiger, and republisher of hard-to-find Nevil Shute novels, expressed an interest in publishing *The Seafarers* as a separate book, the first Nevil Shute book to be newly published in over forty years!

With that impetus, I contacted Jerre Schermerhorn, surely the most dedicated worker the Nevil Shute Foundation has ever known, and asked if she would transcribe the barely legible manuscripts into a more readable word processing format. As has been her response to such requests in the past, she agreed to take on the entire project, without compensation.

With the proofreading aid of my wife Zia, who has found herself involved in more Nevil Shute related work than she ever anticipated when she first considered marrying me, I have edited and accomplished some minor rewrites of Nevil Shute's second version of *The Seafarers*. In doing so, I have maintained the feel of his writing to the best of my ability. After final proofings by Johan Bakker and Shoshana Milgram, two more dedicated Shutists, the novella was ready for publication.

As icing on the cake, Brooke Steiger, an Albuquerque artist, was commissioned to paint the opening scene of *The Seafarers* for use as a dust jacket or book cover illustration for the story. Ms. Steiger used the dust jacket of the first edition Heinemann *Requiem for a Wren* as a conceptual model. Starting with that, she painted a scene to fit the characters and background of *The Seafarers*. The original of this painting is the property of The Nevil Shute Norway Foundation.

It is an honor to have played a part in the first Nevil Shute book to be published since 1961. My heartfelt thanks go out

THE SEAFARERS

THE SEAFARERS
BY
NEVIL SHUTE

WITH AN INTRODUCTION BY
SHOSHANA JOY MILGRAM

Published with permission by:
The Paper Tiger, Inc.
335 Jefferson Avenue
Cresskill, NJ 07626
(201) 567-5620
www.papertig.com

Cover illustration by Brooke Steiger
Book layout by Mark Van Horne

ISBN: 1-889439-32-0

to Jerre Schermerhorn, Zia Telfair, Johan Bakker and Shoshana Milgram for their production assistance; to Fred Weiss for obtaining permission to publish this book, to Brooke Steiger for the excellent cover art, and to the 600 or so Shutists who have given their support, contributed to our Internet site, attended the Centennial and OZ2001 celebrations, and done so much to keep the spirit and philosophy of Nevil Shute Norway alive.

Good on yer!

Dan Telfair
Albuquerque, NM
March 17, 2002

INTRODUCTION

The Seafarers, a novella written by Nevil Shute in the years 1946–47 and published now for the first time, dramatizes one of his most important themes: the life-giving joy of productive work. His own life story exemplifies this very theme. Shute's autobiography, *Slide Rule* (1953), deals with the manifold achievements of his first career (as an aeronautical engineer and as the founder of his own aircraft firm) and with the beginning years of his second career, as a writer. The epigraph to that book cites Robert Louis Stevenson: "the true success is to labour." Shute thus calls attention to the rewards of goal-oriented mental and physical effort, as measured not only after the attainment of the goal, but at every stage of the struggle. In *The Seafarers*, Shute concentrated his considerable powers on analyzing that "true success"—showing how it can be won and how, even if lost, it can be regained.

The story line is elegantly simple. As World War II winds down, Donald Wolfe (a senior naval lieutenant) and Jean Porter (a boat's crew Wren) meet when he brings his motor gunboat to Portland harbor to be dismantled and disarmed. They admire each other's dedication and cheerful competence; their first date is promising, and both hope for a romance. But when they meet again in peacetime, away from the sea, they seem to have much less in common. Without the work they love, their differences are magnified. Puzzled and disappointed, they part, regretfully—but not permanently.

The present book is Shute's second version of *The Seafarers*, written not long after the first, with some enhancements in style and characterization, but no changes in the story line. Although Shute did not choose to publish either version of *The Seafarers*, he returned to several of its elements in two other works: *Blind Understanding*, left incomplete in 1948 and never published, and *Requiem for a Wren* (known in the U.S. as *The Breaking Wave*), published in 1955.

All three titles feature a capable, matter-of-fact young woman who has joined the Wrens fresh from school and developed skills and confidence. When her war service ends, however, she is adrift. The versions are significantly different in three main ways, all of them to the advantage of *The Seafarers*.

To begin with, the heroines of *Blind Understanding* and *Requiem for a Wren*, each named Janet, serve as Ordnance Wrens; each shoots down a plane carrying seven men, who may not in fact belong to the enemy side. The identity of the men killed is never established; it is suggested that Janet committed an error of judgment. Although Shute does not make Janet unequivocally guilty, she blames herself for the seven deaths, and also for the subsequent deaths of her father and her fiancé, which she attributes to divine retribution. Shute left unresolved the story of the heroine of *Blind Understanding*; the story of the heroine of *Requiem for a Wren* ends in tragedy.

In *The Seafarers*, by contrast, the heroine's war work is an unambiguous good. She has learned how to repair and manage boats; she solves practical problems. Jean never has to cope with the possibility of tragic error that is a central focus of the other texts. She has nothing on her conscience, no mysteries to unravel. She mourns no dead. Her skill is an unquestioned asset, and her life is triumphantly un-tragic.

Another feature unique to *The Seafarers* is the characterization of Donald Wolfe, a heroic counterpart to the heroine. In the other versions, the heroine's fiancé dies during the war, and the man who approaches her later (Robert Prentice in *Blind Understanding*, Alan Duncan in *Requiem for a Wren*) is less than direct in his courtship of her. But in *The Seafarers*, Shute creates a character who not only loves and admires the heroine, but who seeks and finds the solution to the problem they share.

The solution to the problem, for Donald and Jean, requires finding in peacetime the purposefulness that was automatically present during the war. *The Seafarers* identifies productive work as the cardinal value of the war years, for both Jean and Donald. The emphasis on work is the third distinctive feature of *The Seafarers*, and the most important. *Blind Understanding* and *Requiem for a Wren*, by contrast, stress the end of youth, the loss of unrepeatable opportunities.

By focusing on work instead of on youth, Jean Porter and Donald Wolfe are able to find in their post-war lives the purposefulness that inspired their war-time happiness. In war, when they worked hard to defeat the enemy, their efforts were richly rewarded—not only by the ultimate military victory, but by the ongoing satisfaction of the struggle (the skills they developed, the challenges they assumed). In order to earn such rewards in peacetime, they must discover for themselves new, and significant, goals.

Turning back the clock, returning to one's youth, serving as a Wren when there is nothing for a Wren to do—all are impossible. But the desire of Donald and Jean—for peacetime work as rewarding as their military service—is open to fulfillment.

That fulfillment, to be sure, is neither quick nor easy. Initially, they follow the paths of least resistance. Donald becomes an insurance agent, like his father, and Jean signs up for secretarial training. The result of their passivity in the selection of goals is predictable. Not only does their work fail to match their abilities, but they have not discovered, or even attempted to discover, a long-range or large-scale purpose comparable to what they were given by the war.

Their arranged meeting in London, months after the war, is a disaster of surprises, misunderstandings, and disappointments. Yet Shute, by making the reader privy to their parallel thoughts, shows that they have more in common than they realize. When they part, we—but not they—know it is not forever.

The lovers are irreplaceable to each other, a fact that Jean, at least, sees intensely when she believes they have said goodbye. "In years to come," Jean reflects, "when time had eased the sharp grief that had come upon her now, there might be other men, but she knew that there would never be another man like Donald." To lose each other would be to miss their best chance of happiness. They do not miss their chance.

In the following chapters, both Donald and Jean find temporary assignments of boat work, tasks other people consider difficult or even impossible. With his trademark descriptive style—understated, detailed, and concrete—Shute makes their endeavors credible, dramatic, and inspiring. They do, in essence, what they did during the war: in the face of danger and discomfort, they exert the mental and physical effort required to achieve important objectives. When Donald and Jean face their challenges, with courage and intelligence, they are—without knowing it—journeying back to each other.

When they find each other again, appropriately "messing about with boats," Jean devises a business plan that will benefit them both. As Wolfe and Porter, Ltd., they convert and sell boats; as Donald and Jean, they live happily ever after. The "true success" of their work, ever increasing in range and scale, will exemplify the epigraph of *Slide Rule*.

The joy of purposeful work, to be sure, is fundamental to Shute. It underlies not only his own experience as an engineer-novelist with two careers, but also many of his other books, notably *Ruined City* (1938) and *Round the Bend* (1951). *On the Beach* (1957) spotlights the power of purposeful work to give meaning to life even when all human life is coming to an end.

The Seafarers is shorter than Shute's published novels. It is uncomplicated by the twists, mysteries, and subplots that enrich his other books. But its simple directness is no defect. Shute gives Jean and Donald, or allows them to give themselves, the only paradise worth having: one joint project after another, in their burgeoning business. They pursue, together, a meaningful life. The dignity of the book eloquently crystallizes the dignity possible to a human being.

In *The Seafarers*, Nevil Shute celebrates the tenacity, intelligence, and drive—in Jean, in Donald, in human nature—that make possible the world of work.

Shoshana Joy Milgram
Blacksburg, Virginia

CHAPTER I

A British naval dockyard is an unattractive place. Even the Wrens, Lieutenant Wolfe thought grimly, were dirty in Portland harbour. He leaned over the windbreak of the little gutted bridge of Motor Torpedo Boat No. 1029, and looked down at the girl in the boat moored alongside. She was about the dirtiest Wren that he had ever seen. Her duffle coat was thin and worn with much service; it was grey with dirt around the cuffs and down the front where it made contact with the dirty warps she handled. The backs of her hands were clean enough, but the palms were black from the same ropes, or from the engine of her boat. There was a smear upon her forehead where she had brushed a wisp of hair back with a dirty hand. She was a mess, like everything else in that place.

He had not been in Portland harbour long. M.T.B. 1029 was his first command. He had had her for eighteen months of war service, operational from Plymouth on the south coast of England. In that eighteen months, he had been in contact seven times with German E-boats in the English Channel; sudden fierce little battles in the night against an enemy who came to him as a blip upon the radar screen and materialized as a vague shadow and a sudden burst of Oerlikon fire. He had sunk one of those shadowy enemies, and damaged several. He had sunk two small coasters slinking down the coast of Normandy in the darkness, one with a torpedo and one with depth charges. If the war had gone on he would have been promoted to lieutenant commander in charge of a flotilla of these little high speed warships, but the war had not gone on.

He had brought M.T.B. 1029 to that ugly, windswept minor dockyard to be disarmed, and for ten days he had been swinging at a buoy in the harbour while the dockyard hands pulled his ship to pieces. His officers and crew had been drafted away to other service or to demobilisation as soon as he reached Portland. He was due for demobilisation in a week or two himself. His present duty was to stay with his ship till her disarmament was finished and then to sail her with a crew drawn from the pool to Chichester, where she would be laid up for disposal. She would be sold for a houseboat to some city worker who feared the sea but liked to be upon it at the week-ends, very safely anchored in a mud creek, floating only at the top of the spring tides. That would be the end of M.T.B. 1029 and her nine battles. He would leave her to be haggled over by the week-enders. In a short time, he would be one of them himself.

In the meantime, he lived alone on board, taking his meals in the wardroom of the base on shore. His tiny cabin aft was still his own, but the rest of his ship was full of dockyard hands; dirty, languid, undisciplined civilians, uninterested in their work or in his ship. Bit by bit, they had taken her to pieces before his eyes. First they had moved her beneath a crane and lifted out her guns and her torpedo tubes. Then they had returned her to the buoy to set about the smaller stuff. As the days followed, they had ripped out all her radio and radar sets, her aerials, her fire control gear, her depth charge carriers, her light gun mountings, the safe for confidential books, and her stoves and mess deck fittings. On the bridge, even her binnacle had gone. In a few days, they had turned his command from a smart warship into a worthless hulk, and his duty had been to stay there and see it done. It was to be his last duty in the Navy.

He spent more time on board than many officers would have done under the circumstances. He had a feeling for ships, and though his ship was being utterly destroyed, it worried him to see her damaged needlessly. Dockyard mateys working in M.T.B. 1029 soon learned that pipes and conduits had to be unscrewed at the unions and not just broken or sawn through. Lieutenant Wolfe had little jurisdiction over them, but he had a sharp tongue. He spent most of those days on board, watching the work, lounging in the cold October wind in the dismantled bridge, morose. He was twenty-five years old and he had been in the Navy for six years, since he left school in 1939. He knew no other way of life.

The dockyard mateys came out each day to his vessel in an L.C.P. driven by a Wren; a dirty boat on dirty work, that carried dirty men and soiled, dismantled gear backwards and forwards to the quay. Inevitably upon this work, the Wren herself was far from smart. She wore a blue seaman's jersey and a pair of dirty blue serge slacks underneath an oil-stained duffle coat. Her hands were usually black with tar and grease from the warps she handled, soaked in the oily scum of the harbour water, or from the engine of her boat, which needed constant humouring. Some of the dirt from her hands transferred itself to her face as the day went on. She usually wore no cap, and the short, fair hair blew round her eyes in the cold wind and got pushed back by dirty hands, so that at times her hair had streaks of dirt upon it too.

Lieutenant Wolfe smiled a little as he looked down at her from the bridge; a domestic servant, or a nursemaid, he thought, snatched into the Navy by conscription and trained to run a boat. He watched her idly for a time. Her boat was made fast alongside, chafing the grey paint that had once been smart, whilst she waited to take the men back to the quay when they knocked off for dinner in an hour's time. She had produced a kettle, a Primus stove and a teapot from some locker, and in the windy bleakness of the cockpit, she was trying to light the Primus to brew a cup of tea. Each time she lit the methylated spirit, it blew out. She gave up presently and tried with paraffin and a small wisp of cotton waste to make a more robust flame. She made one three feet high with clouds of black, greasy smoke and smothered it hurriedly with a wet rag. He heard her swear a good round naval oath as she put a scorched finger hurriedly into her mouth, and he smiled again.

He leaned over the bridge rail. "In the boat, there," he called. "There's a stove here in the wardroom pantry. You can come aboard and brew your tea there, if you like."

She looked up, brushing her hair back with the clean back of her hand. "Oh, thank you, sir," she said. "This filthy thing won't go."

In the social system of the Navy, it was a small act of courtesy upon his part. If his ship had been in commission, he would not normally have asked a Wren rating to the wardroom flat unless he had known her personally. He would have told her to come aboard and go ask the cook for a cup of tea, and she would have gone forward to the mess decks. He watched her as she stuffed the pockets of her duffle coat with tins of tea and milk, and a paper bag of biscuits. After she clambered on board with her kettle, her teapot and her cup, he went down from the bridge and led her below to the small gas ring in the wardroom pantry. "They've taken the big stove," he said, "but this will do all you want."

"It's very kind of you to let me use it, sir," she said. "Shall I make you a cup?"

He hesitated and replied: "I don't know that there's a cup left here."

She said quickly, "I've got another cup down in the L.C.P. I'll bring it to you when it's ready."

"I'll have it down here, out of the wind," he said. "I'll be back presently."

He went on deck and down to the chartroom to see that the echo sounder was being removed with proper respect. Ten minutes later he was back in the wardroom. The kettle was boiling and the girl was making tea. "I hope you don't mind, sir," she said, "but I washed my hands in the basin in your heads. I didn't want to get your cup all over muck."

"That's all right," he said. He glanced at her. She had tidied up her hair and cleaned her face. She had taken off her duffle coat and was moving deftly round the little pantry in her blue jersey, slacks and rubber shoes. He went into his cabin, and took off his bridge coat and muffler. Upon returning to the wardroom, he found tea laid for him alone, with her teapot on the table, her tin of milk, a few lumps of sugar in a saucer, and a plate of chocolate biscuits and petits-beurre. There was no tablecloth because there was no tablecloth left on board, but she had done her best to make it look inviting. He glanced out to the pantry and saw her standing there by the gas ring with her cup of tea and a few biscuits on the draining board. He said, "Won't you bring yours in and have it with me?"

She smiled. "I'll be all right here, sir."

"Don't do that," he said. "Come in and have it comfortably in here."

"All right." She came in and sat opposite to him in the narrow cabin. He took a biscuit. "I haven't seen chocolate biscuits for years," he said. "Where did you get them from?"

"My mother sends them to me, from home," she said.

"They're rationed, aren't they?"

She nodded. "They're on points. But Daddy gets these from some place he does business with or something. I get a parcel of them nearly every week."

"Wish I did."

She laughed. "I have to keep them under lock and key in the Wrennery. I save them to eat in the boat."

"Been here long?"

She told him that she had been at Portland for two years. "It was all right till the war ended," she said. "I mean, when everything was operational and you felt you were really doing something. Now it's pretty foul here. They've reduced the boat's crew Wrens a lot recently. I'm one of the last. There are only five of us left now, in Portland."

She had been in the Navy for three years, in boats all the time. Her group number for demobilisation was in the forties, and she did not expect to be returned to civil life until the spring. With the reduction of the boat's crews she had volunteered for dockyard work rather than risk regrading as a clerk or a steward. "It's pretty foul, this job," she repeated, "but I'd rather finish up as I began, in the boats."

He nodded. "It's a pretty grim time for everybody," he said quietly. "This business of picking the ship to bits gives me the willies. A dockyard always gets me down."

She said impulsively, "Do have another biscuit, sir. I've got heaps."

In spite of his kindness to her, she was rather in awe of him. After three years in the Navy she knew almost by instinct which officers were competent and which were not, with which you could take liberties and with which you must be very correct. She knew that this was one of the officers with whom you had to watch your step in all matters of duty. She learned something of the history of all the vessels that came in for disarmament, and she knew that M.T.B. 1029 had seen more action than most. She knew that this captain and this ship had sunk more than one enemy vessel, and that they had had a very good reputation at Plymouth. The Distinguished Service Cross was not a very common decoration on an R.N.V.R. lieutenant, and she knew the ribbon when she saw it. She had heard Lieutenant Wolfe ticking off the dockyard hands for slovenly work and she had heard them grousing about it in her boat. She knew he had them very well in hand. However they might carry on in other ships, she knew that M.T.B. 1029 would be dismantled carefully and well. She was interested to meet Lieutenant Wolfe. Three years of the Navy had brought her much disillusionment. All naval officers, she had discovered, were not virile, competent, strong minded men as she had thought when she was at school. She had, however, met a few who were, a few who seemed to fulfil all the expectations of her schooldays in their competence and their integrity. Lieutenant Wolfe was one of them, one of the few.

He finished his tea, refused a third biscuit, and got up to go on deck, the echo sounder still upon his mind. "Thanks awfully for the tea," he said.

She smiled shyly. "It's been very good of you to let me come aboard here, sir."

"That's all right," he said. "You can come down here any time you want to use the stove. You can't use that Primus in the boat."

"That's terribly kind of you, sir. It *is* difficult to get it going in this wind. It was all right in the summer."

He nodded. "Well, use this place any time you want."

He went on deck and left her washing up the cups, gratified and impressed by his consideration. Work upon M.T.B. 1029 would carry on for two or three days more. It would be a comfort to her to come on board to brew tea for elevenses and in the afternoon. Moreover, she had enjoyed making tea for him and meeting him, and she looked forward to doing it again. It was quiet in the wardroom flat. She looked around furtively and peeped into his cabin. It was very much like any other officer's cabin. There was a uniform on a hanger on the bulkhead, a pair of blue pyjamas on the bunk, and a few detective stories. On the wall, there was a large framed photograph of a girl which interested her very much. She glanced over her shoulder and went in to investigate it more closely. It was a printed reproduction of a photograph of Rita Hayworth. She smiled with relief, went out, and shut the door behind her.

Wolfe was on deck next morning standing over the welder as he burned the ready-use ammunition lockers off the deck, watching to see that he did not burn through the deck, when the Wren appeared beside him. "Cup of coffee in the wardroom, sir," she said, "or will you have it here?"

"Coffee?" he said. "That's a good idea. I'll be down in a minute."

"Very good, sir."

When he went down to the wardroom he found a small tablecloth laid, white and inviting on the stained table, and a blue cup and saucer, and a plate of rock cakes; all this was new on board. The Wren had heard him coming and he found her pouring out his coffee. He took off his coat. "Been pushing out the boat a bit," he said. "Where did the china come from?"

"I brought it on board from the Wrennery, sir. I'll take it back before you go."

"Okay. Did you have to pay for the cakes?"

"I got them at the N.A.A.F.I."

"I'll give you the money for them."

He made her come and sit down in the wardroom where they drank their coffee together. He noticed that she was cleaner than she had been the previous afternoon, probably in his honour, though it was morning and she had not had so long to get dirty. She was not a particularly glamourous girl, but like all boat's crew girls she was well developed and supremely healthy. There never was a really ugly boat's crew Wren. The physical health that the life brought these girls prevented that. He was pleased to have her with him in the wardroom; it made a break in the monotony of his depression. "What's your name?" he asked.

"Porter, sir. Jean Porter." She had no jacket on to show her rank; she wore her seaman's jersey.

"Leading Wren?" he asked.

"That's right."

He did not now think that she had been either a nursemaid or a domestic servant. "What did you do before you joined the Navy?"

She laughed. "I didn't do anything. I joined straight from school."

He nodded. "So did I." He took a drink of coffee and ate a bit of rock cake. "Blowed if I know what I'm going to do now."

She said, "Won't you go on in the service?" It had not occurred to her that such an officer would be demobilised.

He shook his head. "I put in for a regular commission, but they turned me down."

She was astonished. "What an extraordinary thing!"

"I don't know," he said. "Everybody can't stay in. As a matter of fact, I don't know that I'm altogether sorry. It probably wouldn't be so much fun in peace time."

She nodded. "It might be a bit flat."

"What do you think you'll do?"

"Me? I hadn't thought about it much. I shan't get out for a good long time. But I'll have to get a job of some sort. I don't know what."

"Where'd you live?"

"In Northampton, sir."

He nodded. "I live in Ealing, just on the outskirts of London, to the west."

"I know that," she said. "You go through it on the train on the way down here from London."

He went on deck again presently and left her to wash up the cups. With the removal of the ready-use ammunition lockers, work on the M.T.B. 1029 was coming to an end. Practically everything that could be of any use in any future war had been taken off the ship to be put into store. The only large items of value that remained were her main engines, and they would be removed at Chichester when she had made her last voyage under power. Lieutenant Wolfe went to the office of the Admiral Superintendent of the Dockyard after lunch and was told that work upon the ship would finish at midday next day. He went on to the office of the Commander in Chief to make application for a crew and for a movements order to sail his boat to

Chichester. Those matters kept him upon shore all afternoon and he did not see the Wren again that day.

She made coffee for him again next morning in his ravished, dismantled vessel, and sat with him in the wardroom. "The work's pretty well finished, isn't it?" she asked. "I've got orders to take all the gang to No. 928 this afternoon."

"That's right," he said. "It's all done now. The crew comes aboard tomorrow morning, and I'm sailing her to Chichester. That's the end of it." He relapsed into silence, staring absently at the tablecloth before him.

She said gently, "I shouldn't think you'd be sorry to get away from here."

"No." He turned to her, and she was concerned at the distress that showed in his face. "It's very depressing," he said quietly. "She was such a fine little ship once and so beautifully equipped—we'd got everything. And she did some good work, too. And now—just look at her!"

"I know," she said. "It's an awful shame. They can't keep them all, of course, but it's a pity to see them done in like this."

He smiled ruefully. "She's a regular shambles up on deck. I suppose it doesn't matter now." He turned to her. "I'll probably cut my throat if I stick around here tonight. Would you like to come into Weymouth with me this evening and do a flick, and have dinner somewhere?"

She beamed with pleasure. "I'd like to awfully, sir."

"Well, let's do that," he said. "What time can you get off?"

She said, "I could get myself cleaned up and meet you at the Transport park at seventeen thirty."

"Fine. I'll see the transport officer and see if I can raise a car," he said. They sat together for a time over the coffee making plans for their evening. Then he went on deck again to watch the dockyard hands, to see that no light-fingered gentleman walked off with some small article that should have stayed on board.

He could not raise a service car that evening, so he arranged a taxi and met her with it at the transport yard. For the first time he saw her in her shore-going Wren uniform, clean and neat in her blue coat and skirt, her white collar and tie, and her black rayon stockings. Her seaman's jersey had shown him a good deal of her figure and he had been very conscious of it. He now realised that she was quite a good-looking girl. Up till now he had liked her for her good manners and for her consideration. He had found her easy to talk to, somebody of little account to whom he could unburden himself and talk about his ship. She was still so, but in addition he now saw that she could make herself look very presentable. He would not have to seek a teashop or a cheap café to put her at ease. She had an air of confidence and poise about her. He could take her anywhere.

He took her to the best hotel in the seaside resort, the Gloucester. They sat together at the bar on little red leather and chromium stools and drank a martini, studying the evening paper to choose their movie. Presently, he said, "What about the other half?"

She smiled. "If you're having it, sir."

He turned to her. "Look, don't you think you might cut out that 'sir' stuff? We aren't on duty now. My name is Donald—Donald Wolfe."

She laughed, a little awkwardly. "I'm sorry. One sort of gets in the habit of it. My name's Jean—oh, I believe I told you when you asked if I was a Leading Wren."

He nodded. "You needn't think I'm going to call you Miss Porter all the time. I shall call you Jean."

"All right. Give me another martini, Donald, and I'll remember not to call you 'sir'."

"Loosen up the inhibitions," he said laughing.

They put their heads together over the paper, studying the advertisements of movie shows, and decided to go and see Carmen Miranda. They sat on for half an hour with cigarettes and short drinks as a preparation. Presently she asked, "Have you thought any more about what you're going to do when you're demobbed?"

He shook his head. "I haven't got a clue. I'd like it to be something like this, in the open air, messing about with boats. But everybody wants to do that, of course. My father works in an insurance office in the City. He could get me into that. But that means going to the office every day, and a fortnight's holiday once a year. I think I'd die of it."

"You wouldn't really," she said practically. "My Daddy, he went all through the last war, from 1914 right up to the end. He must have been about the same age as you when he came out. He wanted to go cattle farming in Canada or something, but it didn't come off and he settled down to the office all right. You know, you do, when you've got to."

"I suppose so. What does you father do?"

"He sells leather belting for machines and things like that. He was a major in the Gunners in the last war. That's why he wanted to go to Canada, because he knew about horses."

"He must have been pretty good to be a major."

"I don't know. It's only the same as lieutenant commander with us. You'd have got a half stripe if the war had gone on, wouldn't you, sir?"

"Like hell I would have, madam."

She flushed a little, laughing. "I forgot."

"Have another martini to help you remember."

"No thanks. We'd better go and have some blotting paper if I'm going to see anything of Carmen Miranda. I'm practically seeing double as it is."

"That's all right. Means you'll enjoy the flick twice as much."

They went through into the dining room, laughing, and sat down to dinner. "What'll you do when you get out?" he asked.

"Me? I haven't really thought about it much. I don't think people do until they get demobbed." She paused. "Of course,

I'd like to go on with boats, but I don't suppose it'll pan out that way. I'll have to do something for a living. Some office, I suppose. Some of the Wrens say they're going to take up nursing, but I think I'd loathe that."

He nodded. "You'd have to be keen on it to take up that."

"It might be rather fun to be a receptionist at a hotel," she said thoughtfully.

"I should think that might suit you," he said. He thought, "She's got a nice voice and a good appearance. She could do that all right."

"I think I'll take a course in shorthand typing anyway," she said. "That always helps, in almost any job."

"Bit of a change after the boats."

"I know," she said sadly. "But what else can one do?"

He stared across the room, depressed. "It's not much fun, this Peace," he said quietly. "The office for me, and shorthand typing for you. No more messing about with boats or the sea for either of us, unless we can afford to do it at week-ends. We've had it. There's a good deal to be said for a nice war."

She took him up. "Well, there is. I'd never have learnt any of the things I've learnt in the last three years if there hadn't been a war."

"Nor would I," he replied. "I'd have gone into the office when I was eighteen and stayed there. The war was a bit grim at times, but one did get around and see things. And places, and people."

Jean said, "I think war's a good thing for people like us, if it doesn't bump you off."

"The way I'm feeling now, I rather wish it had."

"Save a lot of trouble," she agreed. "Still, it won't be so bad as all that. I thought life in the Wrens would be terrible before I went in, but I've enjoyed it, on the whole. I expect we'll like the Peace all right when we get used to it."

"I hope so," he remarked.

The girl said firmly, "Well, we've darned well got to. I remember hearing Daddy sounding off one day about all the old soaks in Northampton who were in the last war, Major This and Captain That, who weren't good enough to hold a job and stuck around the pubs all day selling carpet sweepers and second-hand cars on half commission. They couldn't make a living in the Peace and so they thought the last war was the tops. Just because they weren't any good in themselves, really."

He grinned. "That's me in five years time."

She said, "It's nothing of the sort. You'll get on all right."

"I'm blowed if I know what at." He turned to her. "The trouble with me," he said quietly, "is that I'm just not interested in anything except boats and the sea. I'm twenty-five years old, and I've been doing this for the last six years. I know that's not a great age, but I think you get old quicker in the war. I think it's more like being thirty-five in peacetime. I do know something about boats and the sea. I feel like a chap of thirty or thirty-five who's got to start and work up interest in another kind of job. It's not so good, you know."

She said, "You'll make out all right, Donald." But now there was a touch of uncertainty in her voice, and in her mind.

"I'm sure I hope so," he said heavily. "But I wish to goodness there was something I could find to do at sea."

"Well, isn't there, if you feel like that about it?" She paused, and then said, "What about the Merchant Service? Couldn't you go into that?"

"I did think of that," he said. "But—I don't know. I haven't got any certificates and it'd take a long time to work up and get them all. And I've not got a lot of money," he said candidly. "I'll have to get to earning something pretty quick."

"Surely you can get those while you're working as a mate, or something."

"Maybe. But anyway, it's not the sort of sea that I'm accustomed to. I want something to do with small boats, like I'm used to now. I wouldn't want to be mate of a tramp steamer and live in Birkenhead."

She smiled. "I think you're a bit particular," she said.

"I suppose I am." He grinned. "It just can't be, and that's all about it. I'll end up in a city office, like the other stiffs."

"You aren't the only one," the girl said. "I'll probably end up like that myself."

He glanced at her. "You'll get married."

She shrugged her shoulders. "Possibly," she said indifferently. "But it's a bit grim to finish up like that just because you're fed up with your job."

"Most girls seem to like it all right."

She smiled. "I never thought I'd feel so lost when the time came to leave the Navy," she remarked. "It's going to be awful. I don't know what I'll do."

They finished their dinner and went out. As he helped her into her coat in the hotel lobby, he was thrilled by the touch of her shoulders and the faint aroma of her powder. She had become very far removed from the dirty rating who drove the L.C.P. with dockyard mateys to his ship. She had turned into a friendly and attractive girl, somebody with whom he could share his troubles. He was most conscious of her attraction as they walked side by side to the cinema, officer and rating. He would have liked to wash out the cinema and take her to a dance instead, but he could hardly suggest that. They went to Carmen Miranda, and sat in the warm darkness elbow to elbow laughing together for three hours. When they came out into the cold, windy street they had become firm friends.

They found a taxi with some difficulty, and set out on the five-mile drive back to the dockyard. In the dim stuffiness of the cab she turned to him. "I have enjoyed this evening, Donald," she said. "I don't know when I've had so much fun."

"I'm glad," he said simply. "We've not done much, though— just dinner and the pictures."

"I know," she said. "But it's been lovely."

In the dim light of a passing street lamp he glanced at her. "It's a shame I've got to go away tomorrow," he said. "We might have fixed up to go to a dance, or something. How long do you think you'll be here for?"

She shrugged her shoulders. "I don't know. I believe they're packing up the boat's crews altogether here. I put in to go to Germany the other day."

"In boats?"

"Oh yes, in boats, just the same. They're sending some Wrens over to run boats at Hamburg and at Kiel."

He said carefully, because he was not very good at lying, "I've got an aunt in Dorchester I ought to go see some time. I might be down this way after I get demobbed, while I'm on my fifty-six days' leave. If you're still here, would you like to come out with me in my civvy suit?"

She was convinced that he had no such aunt; mischievously, she would have liked to pull his leg about it, to ask her name and where she lived, to say that she herself had lived in Dorchester and knew everybody there. But the time had not yet come for that, she thought. She said, "I'd love to. Some of the suits are quite good, aren't they?"

"Some are just terrible," he said. "It depends a lot which depot you are sent to for demob."

"We don't get an issue of clothes, like you do," she said. "We get money given us instead. I believe you do better out of it."

They came to the dockyard gate and got out into the windy darkness. There was a light rain falling. He paid off the taxi and they stood together for a few moments, reluctant to part. "You will be sure and write and let me know when you come down here, won't you?" the girl asked.

"I will indeed." He fumbled in his pocket for a pencil and a scrap of paper. "Tell me, what's your number?" As a rating it would be necessary for him to put her service number into the address.

She said, "Six seven four eight five three, sir. Leading Wren J. Porter, six seven four eight five three."

He wrote it down, grinning. "All right, madam."

She laughed, embarrassed at her mistake. "I've had to give that number so many times—on duty, I mean. I'm sorry."

He said, "Well, there won't be any more of that in a week's time—with me." There was uncertainty in his voice, and a little bitterness, perhaps even a little fear.

She said softly, "It'll be all right. You'll see."

"I suppose it will. Let's keep up, if we can."

In the dim light from the guardroom lamp he put out his hand, and she took it, and they stood hand in hand for a few moments. "I wish we'd gone to a dance tonight instead of to the pictures," he said.

"Never mind," she said gently. "We can do that another time."

"I'll write and let you know." He grinned at her. "The sentry's very interested in us," he said. "Eyes popping out of his head. We'd better break it up. Good night, Jean."

"Good night, Donald."

CHAPTER II

Donald Wolfe sailed for Chichester next day, his last voyage in the Navy. He left his ship and went to Portsmouth to the Royal Naval Barracks; three days later he was passed through the demobilisation routine. His civilian clothes were made up into a carton and carrying this, he travelled up to London. Fifty-six days leave upon full pay lay ahead of him; after that he would be finally and irrevocably out of the Navy. He felt very much at a loss, and rather afraid of the new life ahead.

He travelled down from London in a suburban electric train, and walked a quarter of a mile from the station to the small house where his father and mother lived, carrying his carton of issue clothes and his suitcase. His parents were not very well off, and they never would be. They lived in a small three-bedroom house in a row. Before the war they had employed a young girl as a maid, but she had been called up, and with the wartime rise in wages, they had been without help for three years. Donald's father was a clerk in a great insurance office in Holborn, a grey-haired, serious-minded man who never missed the eight forty-two train to the office, nor failed to arrive home on the six thirty-seven. He was a great gardener. He entered his sweet peas each year for the Ealing Horticultural Show, and talked about them at the office for the following year to anybody who would listen to him.

His father and mother were very glad to see Donald home again, if somewhat puzzled by him. There was another son who had been in the Army, killed in Libya in 1941; there was a daughter married to a traveller in porcelain ware and bathroom fittings, who lived near Wolverhampton. Donald was their last child at home. When he had left them to join the Navy in 1939 he had been an easy, pliable boy, ready to fall in with the plans his father had made for him and to grow up in their way of life. Six years in the Navy had turned him into something they admired very much, but did not understand. They had been terribly proud of him in officer's uniform and thrilled with his Distinguished Service Cross and its investiture by the King at Buckingham Palace. Now the time had come to put off his uniform, and D.S.C.'s were at a discount. They were puzzled and rather disconcerted by what remained of their son when these things were removed.

To Donald, his home and the suburban street seemed narrow, cramped, and confined. He was accustomed to go on deck to a wide view of sea and sky, and had been for six years. The suburb made him feel constrained. The little house seemed small and drab and pokey to him after the spaciousness of wardrooms in a naval barracks, and the hot water supply totally inadequate. He could not sit and see his mother wash the dishes after a meal without helping, and he disliked washing dishes very much indeed, never having had to do it in his life before. Moreover, for the first time in six years he had nothing to do. For a week he found this pleasant; then boredom grew upon him, not relieved by the necessity to look for work. The type of work available to him was just as boring as his leisure.

His father exercised a gentle, insistent pressure on him to go into the insurance business. "It's done very well for me," he said with quiet pride, oblivious to the higher flights of fortune. "You work regular hours, very regular. Half past five I get away each night, regular as a clock. I don't suppose I have to stay late at the office more than twice a year. And regular raises, too; I go up ten pounds a year every Christmas, starting twenty-two years ago, all through the war and everything. And then to top it all, a pension at the end, at sixty-five. I've been very well satisfied with the insurance business, very well satisfied indeed." The prospects did not satisfy his son, but he could find nothing better.

Donald Wolfe knew few people of his own age in Ealing. Most of his school friends had left the district or else were still in the service. In those difficult weeks of readjustment he thought a great deal about Leading Wren Jean Porter. She was somebody friendly and approachable to whom he would talk freely, and he wanted somebody like that very much. The Wren herself was in the same boat; she, too, would soon be out of the Navy and, like him, commencing ruefully to train herself for life in the office. He had been home for barely three weeks before he wrote to her, saying that he would have to visit Dorchester before long and suggesting that they should meet again in Weymouth. It was a fortnight before he got an answer, to his intense anxiety, and then it came from Hamburg. After telling him all about life in occupied Germany, she wrote:

"I'm expecting to get out in time for Christmas now. They've speeded up our demob and all the boats here are being taken over by men. They make an awful mess of things, but I suppose they'll learn. Some of them don't seem ever to have been in a boat before, and they can't even chuck a heaving line or steer a course. I'll have to go home first of all, of course, but it would be awfully nice to meet in London some time after that. I expect I shall be down there looking for a job after Christmas. But I know Mummy will want to have me at home for a bit first, so it won't be till the end of January or some time like that. Let's plan to meet then."

At the end of November Donald Wolfe took a clerk's job in a marine insurance office in a city street not very far from Lloyds. In that atmosphere of debit notes and reinstatement premiums he set to work to try to live on six pounds ten a week, of which one pound went on travelling and another on lunches and the best part of a third on income tax. He found the work every bit as uninspiring as he had feared it might be, and he became much worried over money. He could not bring his living expenses down to the standard of his earning capacity, and the thought that he was eating into his small capital of savings and gratuity perplexed and worried him. He became depressed with a sense of frustration at the thought that he could not earn sufficient to maintain the standard of living he had grown accustomed to.

Leading Wren Jean Porter returned from Germany and was demobilised at Portsmouth on December 18th. She travelled up to Northampton next day, still in her Wren uniform. She was the second of three daughters, the eldest of whom was married, the youngest still in the W.A.A.F. in far Colombo. She had sent a telegram to her mother to tell her the time her train would arrive.

It was a great day for her father and mother, almost as great as it was for the girl herself. Her mother hurried to the kitchen to see the cook and tell her all about it. In the kitchen everybody was innocently delighted at the news.

"Miss Jean was always very partial to the curried chicken, madam," said the cook.

Her mother said, "Oh yes, and we must have the chocolate soufflé, and then mushrooms on toast."

The houseparlourmaid said, "She *does* like mushrooms on toast, madam."

Her mother hurried out to see the gardener and tell him all about it, because of the flowers, and then she sent for the chauffeur. He was an ex-petty officer from the Navy and so had a particularly soft spot for Jean. He came beaming all over his fat face, because the cook had already told him the news. Mrs. Porter said, "Cox, Miss Jean is coming home on the three-thirty; she's demobilised at last."

He said, "That's great news, madam."

She said, "Oh, isn't it? Cox, we shall want the car this afternoon, the Rolls Royce, not the little car. Half past two, and then we'll go and fetch Mr. Porter from the office and go on to the station. And Cox, be sure and have the car looking very nice for her."

He said, "How would it be to have a little decoration on the radiator, madam? We've got some of that red, white and blue ribbon, what we had on Victory day."

She said, "Oh yes, Cox—That'd be fun!"

Mr. and Mrs. Porter drove up to the station that afternoon in considerable style. The day was sunny and bright and the decorated Rolls Royce driven by the smart, fat, beaming Mr. Cox attracted a good deal of attention. Her father and mother met Jean on the platform. She flew out of the train into their arms. "Oh, Daddy and Mummy, it's simply lovely to be home again," she cried.

They kissed her warmly. "Are you really out now, darling, for good?" her mother asked.

"Really out now, Mummy," she said. "No more Navy."

"Oh my darling, I *am* glad for you," her mother said. "It's been such a terrible time for you, and it's been so long."

Jean said, "It hasn't been as terrible as all that, Mummy. It's been a bit long, that's all." And then, as they walked to the station yard, she saw Cox standing by the decorated Rolls. "Oh, there's Cox! Afternoon, Chief. I do like the car—it's frightfully tiddley. Did you do all that for me? How's Mrs. Cox—and Dorothy?"

They got into the great car and drove off through the town. Mrs. Porter touched the rough serge on her daughter's sleeve. "This terrible uniform," she said. "You must be longing to be out of it."

Jean looked down at her clothes. "I've got so accustomed to it now one hardly thinks about it."

The mother smiled at her child's bravery. "It's over now, darling," she said. "Now we must see about getting you some pretty things to wear, and have done with all this horrible coarse serge."

"They've given me a lot of clothing coupons," Jean told her, "but I don't know how far they'll go."

"Don't you worry your head about coupons," said her father heartily. "You just make out a list of what you think you'll want, you and your mother between you. I'll put Dawson onto it, down at the office. It'd be a rum do if we couldn't find you what you want, after three years in the Navy."

Porter and Simmonds, Ltd. made leather and balata belting, as Jean had told Donald Wolfe. In the naval scene it simply had not occurred to her as relevant that they made it for practically every factory in England and the British Empire, and it had never entered her head to tell him that her father was the Chairman and Managing Director of the business. These matters did not seem important to her, engrossed as she had been in naval work. Her life before she joined the Navy had been a life of boarding school and a pleasant country home, a home where various comforts appeared as they became necessary without apparent effort upon anybody's part. When she was of an age to have a pony, a pony had materialised; when new clothes were needed they appeared. The war and the conscription that it brought had prevented her from fully realising that her father was a wealthier man than most. In wartime England there was not much to distinguish the life of a wealthy girl from those of common clay. She had never had more than a pound or two in her purse; as a schoolgirl she had had little use for money, and her parents had been wise enough not to thrust it on her while she was a Wren, fearing to impair her status with her fellows. Instead, they had been content to send her gifts of rayon stockings and chocolate biscuits gleaned from the business of leather belting for machines.

Such gleanings were too easy. Porter and Simmonds, Ltd., making belting as they did for every chocolate and rayon stocking machine in England, inevitably received a number of small presents from the buyers of the belts. When Mr. Dawson, the chief salesman of the company, got the list of clothes from

Mrs. Porter, he had only to lift his telephone, ring the appro-
priate factory, and breathe a word that Mr. Porter's daughter
was demobbed after three years in the Navy. "What about a
length of the peach rayon, or a couple of pairs of them blocked
shoes you showed me last time I was over at your place, or a
set of undies, or a bit of pastel blue silk stuff for an evening
dance frock. Put the samples in the post? Say, old man, that's
very helpful. I'll take them out and let Mrs. Porter see them,
'n let you know." Jean found herself at the end of January with
a very comprehensive wardrobe of the smartest clothes, and
most of her clothing coupons still unspent.

It was her mother's delight to take her in hand and "make
her look presentable". In those first weeks of rest after three
years in the boats, the girl was content to relax and let herself
be polished. In most industrial cities there were shops to cater
for the needs of wealthy women, and in Northampton, Mad-
ame Eloise conducted no mean beauty parlour. Here Jean spent
many hours. It was pleasant in those first cold January weeks
after three Januaries spent in open boats, to sit warm and snug
while deft hands did things to your hair or gently smoothed
your face or trimmed your finger nails, while you read *Punch*
or *Vogue*. It was pleasant to sit so and think of trying to light a
Primus stove in the cold salty wind and dirt; even the touch of
nostalgia that accompanied such thoughts was pleasant in itself.

As the weeks went on, this nostalgia became more trouble-
some. There came a time when all the clothes were bought
and all the beauty possible had been attained, for the moment
at any rate. Over tea one day the girl said to her mother,
"Mummy, I'll have to think about getting a job soon."

Her mother, troubled, looked at her. "What kind of a job,
darling?"

"I don't know. But I can't just sit at home here, living on
you and Daddy."

"My darling, what an extraordinary way to look at things. We love to have you home again—it's been so dull for us with no young people in the house."

Jean said impulsively, "It's sweet of you to say that, Mummy. But honestly, I think I ought to do something and not just sit at home."

"You mean a half time job, dear—doing something for Starving Europe, or something like that?"

"I did mean a real job, Mummy. Whole time."

"But darling," her mother said, "if you did that you wouldn't have time for anything else. I was thinking we might have a dance next month; there are a lot of young people back out of the forces now. We could have Roy Whitfield and his band; they're very good."

"I want to do a job of some kind, Mummy."

Her mother sighed. One daughter had left home for marriage and another one was still in Colombo; it was hard to lose the only one at home. "We'll talk it over with your father, dear, and see if he can suggest something."

She talked it over with him in their bedroom that night, out of hearing of the girl. "Of course," she said with a sigh, "I suppose it's only natural. Jean has her own life to lead, and she's been independent now for so long. But I did hope we could have kept her with us, just for a little while."

"What does she want to do?" he enquired.

"I don't know—I don't think she really knows herself. She just talks vaguely about getting a job. Could she do anything for you down at the office, dear?"

He screwed up his face in distaste. "I dunno. I'd sooner she was in somebody else's office. Better for her, and better for the office."

"I was thinking, dear, if she was in the business, she could take time off now and then, if there was anything really important that she had to do."

"That's what I was thinking of," he said unhelpfully. "If she's going to carry on that way I'd sooner she was in somebody else's office and not mine."

He talked to Jean in the morning. "Your Ma tells me you want to try and get a job," he said kindly.

She smiled. "That's right, Daddy. I can't just sit around at home and wait for somebody to come along and marry me."

"No, I suppose not." He thought about it for a minute. "Any idea what you want to do?"

She shook her head. "I did think I might be a receptionist for a doctor or something like that. Receptionist and secretary."

"Never done any typing or anything o' that, have you?"

She shook her head. "We didn't do that at school."

"Blowed if I know what girls do learn at school," he grumbled. "The more you pay the less they teach. I'd reckon that'd be the first thing, anyway."

She started work at the Northampton Commercial College next week. She was the oldest in a class of about forty fifteen-year-old girls. She was only twenty-one, but already her reaction times were slower than those of the schoolgirls she sat with. It troubled her to find that she was the slowest in the class. Three years in the boats had not fitted her for office work, and it worried her. She very soon became doubtful whether she would ever work up to the speed and accuracy that she knew the best jobs would demand, and more than doubtful if she really wanted such a life.

Spring came early that year in Northampton. As she worked at her cyphers in the crowded classroom, her mind wandered sometimes to the sunlight and blue water, to the vigour of grey skies and the bitter taste of salt spray on her face. The life she was preparing for was less attractive to her way of thinking than the one that she had left, for all that it promised of more comfort and stability. She thought more and more often of the boats, or Portland, of the Wrens' mess and the good company that she had left forever. From time to time she received letters from Wren friends now in civil life again. Some were married, some were back in their former jobs, some were preparing themselves for a new job, as she was. Most of these letters breathed the same nostalgia for the service, the same wistful regret for what was past. The war had been a very good time for these girls, for some of them, the high spot of their lives.

Distant fields are always green. The irritation of discipline and the infuriation she had felt at the stupidities of ageing naval officers, were fading from her mind; she remembered rather the good fellowship of the boats, and the competence and the integrity she had encountered in a few young officers. Her memory of the Navy became crystallised about the figure of Donald Wolfe, the pleasant, depressed young man who wore the D.S.C. and who was watching his ship pulled to pieces and seeing that the work was done carefully and well. The kind young man, who had told her that she might use the wardroom to make tea in, who had taken her to the pictures and, in spite of evident attraction, had not made one pass at her. In her restlessness at home and in her boredom in the shorthand typing class, her thoughts turned more and more to Donald Wolfe, the embodiment of everything that she respected in the Navy. With him, she felt, she could recapture something of the peace of mind that she had left behind her in the service. And Donald Wolfe had written to her once, wanting to take her out again. She had his home address. She sat down one evening in the privacy of her bedroom, in her expensive dressing gown lined with white fur, and wrote a little note to Donald. She said she had to come to London in a week or so, and what about meeting one evening?

Her letter caught him at a time of deep depression; city life was more unpleasant than he had thought possible, and he was very nearly through with washing up at home. For a month he had been looking for rooms of his own, and he could find no way of living that was at the same time within his means and suitable to his ideas. Frustration enmeshed him and weighed him down; the letter from the Wren came to him as a light in the darkness. Here was a chance, he felt, to talk freely to someone, to unburden himself and talk it out. Hitherto he had kept his difficulties to himself. He could not talk them over with his parents or with any of his friends, or with the few superior young women he had met in Ealing. The Wren was different, the dirty little girl who had made tea for him. One could talk to her. He replied enthusiastically to her letter.

In their bedroom two nights later Mrs. Porter said to her husband, "Jean wants to go to London for a couple of days."

He grunted. "You going up with her?"

"No dear. I think she wants to go alone."

"What for?"

"She hasn't said, but I think there's a young man. She said she'd had an invitation to a theatre from somebody she knew in the Navy."

"Of course it's a man, then—she wouldn't be invited by a girl. Any idea who he is?"

"No dear. I thought it better not to ask, until she volunteers something."

He nodded. "After all, she's getting on for twenty-two." The age of their children was a perpetual matter of surprise to them. "She must have been out with a good many young men when she was in the Navy."

His wife said, "It's dreadful to feel they're all getting so old."

He kissed her clumsily. "Where's she going to stay?"

She was silent for a moment. "Do you know, I never thought about that."

"Has she ever stayed in London alone before?"

"Oh, I don't think so. She has stayed in London once or twice, but that was when she was in the Navy and she went to a Wrennery in Hampstead or somewhere. She's never stayed alone in a hotel."

He thought about it for a minute. "She's stayed with us at the Savoy, though."

"Oh yes, she knows the Savoy."

He said, "Get her to go there, then. She'll be quite all right there by herself. I'll ring up Jules and ask him to look after her for me." He was well known at the Savoy Hotel, where they were very careful to keep tabs on their more wealthy clientele.

His wife sighed comfortably. "Oh, that'll be nice, dear. I'll be quite happy in my mind if Jules is looking after her."

Three days later Donald Wolfe got a letter from his dirty little Wren. He did not care to open it before his parents. He read it in the crowded stuffiness of the Underground train to the City. It ran:

Dear Donald,

I'd love to meet you and do a theatre. I haven't seen anything that's on now except Arsenic and Old Lace. I've got to come to town on Friday of next week; could we fix up to do something together on Saturday evening? I shall be staying at the Savoy Hotel. Give me a ring there on Friday night or Saturday morning early, because I've got to go out and do some shopping.

I'm looking forward to hearing all your news.

Yours,

Jean Porter

He read this letter from his Wren in the clamour of the train, and his jaw dropped. The Savoy Hotel . . .

CHAPTER III

Jean Porter travelled up to London by train from Northampton in a pleasant twitter of anticipation. She had enjoyed her evening with Donald Wolfe when she had been a boat's crew Wren and he had been the captain of a motor torpedo boat. She had remembered it throughout the six months with recurrent pleasure. Now that they were about to repeat it, she was looking forward to it very much, and resolved to do everything she could to make their evening a success.

Thinking back to those first meetings in the boats moored off the dockyard, she was amazed and rather gratified to think that he had asked her out at all. He had seen her at her very worst, in filthy working kit, her hands black with grease from the dirty warps she handled, smears of black dirt on her face from brushing her hair back, oil and tar and mud all over her clothes. Those were the circumstances in which they had first met, in which he had asked her out to dinner and a flick. She grinned, reflecting that she must have a good bit of glamour to outweigh all that.

This time she would not have to submit to any disadvantages of that sort. This time there would be no dirty, grease stained uniform to contend with. She was very conscious that her clothes were right. She had two evening frocks with her, one a very lovely thing in pale green and black silk with a long flowing skirt. She had a pair of jade earrings set in silver to go with that, and a jade ring. The other was a short dance frock, pastel blue and silver and with practically no back, and she had some marvellous white silk stockings to go with it, and shoes to match. All these had been gleaned for her by her father's salesman in the business, and he had done his gleaning well.

Donald had written her a short note to say that he would ring her up at the Savoy on Friday evening, and she rode in a taxi there from the station in the middle of the afternoon. She had never stayed alone in London before. She had been to the Savoy with her parents once or twice and knew the rooms, but she had never before stayed alone in any hotel. The war had filled the years since she left school, and as a Leading Wren you did not stay in London hotels. She had passed through London once or twice on duty in those years, and for a moment she had a faint twinge of nostalgia for the Wrennery at Hampstead where she had been accommodated. But there would be no more Wrenneries for her.

She found things unexpectedly easy at the Savoy. As soon as she said her name at the reception desk an assistant manager came out and welcomed her. "We have your room all ready for you, Miss Porter—on the second floor, looking out over the river. I hope you'll like it."

She was not to know that her father, who had used the hotel for twenty years and had spent many hundreds of pounds in it, had rung up Mr. Jules from Northampton and had confided in him that his daughter was visiting London for the first time alone, and would he see that everything was quite all right for her? Jean was gratified and pleased at the attention that was shown to her, and beamed so genially at the assistant manager that she put him into quite a flutter, accustomed though he was to lovely women. She walked from the elevator to her room like a princess. No more Wrenneries.

Her room delighted her. Not only was it warm and airy and well furnished, and with a beautiful bathroom, but the wide window overlooked the river, and she could see ships from it. She had not seen a ship since she had left the Navy and she had missed them, how much she did not know until she saw them again. But there they were, in the grey evening light. There was a motor ship with no masts laden with coal for the Gas Light and Coke Company going up the river beneath bridges. There was a tug with a great string of lighters towing upstream on the flood. There was a hard chine motor launch of the river police and a small open boat, painted and dirty, sailing with a lug sail under the far shore. She knew them all, their types and their technique, what they did and how they did it. It was as if from that window in the Savoy Hotel she could look out at her past life, and nostalgia for what was gone forever swept over her again. Then there was a soft knock on the door and a maid entered, unpacked her pretty clothes for her, and drew the curtains to shut out the grey evening mists, and Jean was back in the warm, cosy peacetime world again.

She had told nobody that she was coming to London, wanting to keep herself quite free for Donald, and so she was somewhat at a loose end that evening. She went downstairs and had tea by herself in the lounge, and then she bought a novel at the bookstore and went up to her room again to wait for his telephone call. She drew aside the curtains and peered out into the darkness. The river was still there; she could see the faint outline of the other shore, with an occasional light. Presently she saw the green sidelight of a vessel going upstream, watched it till its arc became obscured, and let the heavy curtain fall back with a little sigh. No more Navy now. She settled down to read her novel about Love in the Napoleonic Wars.

Donald Wolfe rang her up at about seven o'clock from the R.N.V.R. Club. He was very uncertain in his mind when he rang her. He did not now know how he was to talk to her. It had been a great shock to him when she had written to say that she would be staying at the Savoy. The girl that he had taken out at Portland had been a Wren rating, and rather a dirty one at that. He had liked that. She had been a girl of no pretensions, somebody to whom he could talk freely without difficulty or awkwardness. If he had had the least idea that she was a wealthy girl he would never have talked to her about his money troubles, about his troubles over his job, as he had done. He was in deeper trouble now. He had wanted to talk to her again about his difficulties, but she was staying at the Savoy. With an effort, he adjusted his mind to the idea that she must be very well off. If that were so, he could not talk to her about his money troubles, or even about his unsatisfactory job. One didn't bleat out all that sort of thing to wealthy girls. But if one didn't, what the hell was he going to talk to her about? He felt like an actor who has had his lines changed at the dress rehearsal.

Thinking of his money difficulties, the Savoy was going to take a bit of living up to. He had reckoned to take her to the back of the dress circle and give her dinner in Soho, spending about a couple of pounds in the evening and having a grand time. That did not fit in with Savoy standards. He hastily changed his seats for stalls and booked a table at the Dorchester. The evening was clearly going to cost him about two weeks' salary, which didn't help.

When the telephone bell rang in her bedroom, she got up quickly and took up the receiver. The operator asked her if she would speak to Mr. Wolfe, and she said, "Yes, please." There was a click, and she heard his voice.

"Is that Miss Porter?"

She said, "Hullo Donald. This is Jean."

He said with an exuberant heartiness which was not as she remembered him, "Hullo Jean, it's grand to hear you again. How did you like Germany?"

She said, "Oh, it was pretty foul. Not much better than Portland."

He said jovially, "Well, that was foul enough. Look, I've got a couple of stalls for *Perchance to Dream* for tomorrow night—is that all right? You haven't seen it?"

"I haven't seen it," she replied. "That sounds simply lovely. What time shall we meet, and where?"

"I'll call for you with a taxi about half past six."

"I'll be ready. How are you getting on, Donald?"

He said genially, "Oh, I'm doing fine." He hesitated. "Tell you all about it tomorrow."

"Okay," she said. "See you then."

They rang off, and she sat down with a tiny frown upon her face, vaguely disturbed. It had not been like talking to the quiet rather depressed officer that she had grown fond of at Portland, the man who could make the dockyard mateys obey his will, the man who wore a D.S.C. and yet needed her help. It had not been like talking to him at all. The voice was possibly the same, but there was too much confidence and bonhomie about it now to fit in with the picture of the man that she had treasured all these months. She went in the elevator to dinner uneasy, and a little bit damped. Things never lived up to your expectations, she thought ruefully. Was Donald going to turn out just another man?

She went out alone to a movie, and went early to bed. She was unused to sleeping in an air-conditioned room and disliked the idea, so she threw open the window and let in the cold river mist. All through the night the foghorns of the boats upon the river broke her sleep. She would half rouse, smile, and settle back to sleep again, thinking of boats and how you handled them, of the men you met in them, of Donald. She slept long and pleasantly, if not well.

She got up next morning after breakfast in her bed, full of plans for the evening. She wanted to look respectable for Donald, as she put it to herself, and her few weeks at home under her mother's care had given her a very clear idea of what you did to make yourself look respectable. You went to a beauty parlour and sat there and had the whole works, and you came out three hours later looking radiant. She had had the forethought to make an appointment with a parlour in Duke Street for the forenoon, and she came out at lunch time about seven pounds the poorer and feeling on top of the world. She looked like something straight out of the advertisement pages of *Eve*. Nobody who had known her as a boat's crew Wren could possibly have recognised her. That evening, Donald didn't.

He came into the hotel lobby in his demobilisation raincoat over his demobilisation suit and carrying his demobilisation hat, saw the Hall Porter look at him, and felt awkward. It had been all right going to places like the Savoy in uniform while the war was on, but in civilian clothes you had to be so darned smart. He asked at the desk for Miss Porter's room and they rang up to it, but she was waiting for him within sight, back in the lounge. She saw him standing at the desk as they telephoned her room, and she got up and walked across to him. He saw her coming and looked straight past her. She had to stop by him and say, "Hullo, Donald."

He started, turned, and looked at her. He did not recognise her even then, but very quickly thought, "Christ, this must be her!"

He smiled awkwardly, and said, "Hullo, Jean. I wasn't expecting you to be down here. I was just ringing your room."

She said, "I don't believe you recognised me."

"Well, you do look a bit different to what you looked like in the boats," he admitted. She was delicately made up as to her face and hair and fingernails; she was wearing a short fur evening cape over her green and black silk evening dress; and she wore the jade earrings in her ears and the jade ring on her hand. "It's the uniform that makes the difference," he said. "The only difference between girls in uniform is their faces, so you notice those particularly. But in civvy clothes there's so much else to distract the eye."

She laughed. "I don't believe you'd have known me anyway in uniform," she said.

"I'd have known you in uniform, or in a boat." He paused, and then said, "Have I changed much?"

"Not much. I knew you when you came in." She had, and her heart had sunk a little. His face had been the same, a little more deeply lined, perhaps, but the clothes he wore were so obviously ready-made, and rather worn at that. It looked as if he had no other overcoat but that demobilisation thing, as if he wore that every day. Later on, when he took off his overcoat and showed his suit, she came to the same conclusion about that.

They went out to the taxi and drove to the theatre; on the way he laboured to make bright small talk to her about the weather and demobilisation and the Russians. He was very shy of her and her fur cape and her jade earrings; she did not seem to be his kind of a young woman at all. He could never live up to her on six pounds ten a week earned in an insurance office. It seemed to him that she was right out of his class. He had been prepared for that from the very fact that she was staying at the Savoy, but his disappointment was not the less keen, now that he was with her and felt something of her old attraction. He had wanted desperately to talk over his troubles with the girl that he had taken out in Weymouth, the Wren who had made tea for him and who had known her place so well that she had found it difficult to have her tea with him, the girl who was continually forgetting and calling him 'Sir.' But that girl was not this one.

Jean made the first approach. When they had settled into their seats and read the programme and were listening to the overture, she said, "Tell me about yourself, Donald. What are you doing now?"

He said quickly, "Oh, I'm doing fine. I've got a job with Minchin and Bowater in the City."

"Is that insurance?" she asked.

He nodded. "Marine insurance. I'm finding it much more interesting than I thought it would be."

He spoke too confidently, and she felt instinctively that there was something wrong, that he was lying to her. She asked, "Is it a good job? Is the pay all right?"

"Fine," he said. "More than I was getting in the Navy." She knew that he was lying to her again, and she felt hurt and affronted, remembering their candid talk in the old days. And suddenly there came the sick, penetrating thought that perhaps he might be lying to her because of her fur cape, and her jade earrings, and her room at the Savoy, and her expensive beauty. He had not lied to her when she had been a Wren.

"I'm awfully glad," she said quietly, and sat in silence.

The curtain went up and saved her from the necessity of any further conversation, but she saw nothing of the play. The knees of his demobilisation suit, which she could see without studying him too closely, were already shiny; he must be too hard up to get another. Her silk clad knee beside them was offensively well dressed; she ought to have come out with him in a coat and skirt. In the taxi he had said gaily that he had booked a table at the Dorchester, but could he afford the Dorchester? They should be going somewhere cheaper. But she could not possibly suggest that at this stage; she did not know him nearly well enough for that. She stared at the stage in a sudden wave of misery. This evening, that she had looked forward to so much and made such preparations for, was going wrong.

It went no better as the hours went on; rather they seemed to diverge more from each other. In an interval of the show he asked her what she was doing and she told him about the class in shorthand typing that she was attending, but what she said was biased by her evening frock, her fur cape, and her carefully tended beauty. Donald Wolfe was no fool, and though women had not played a great part in his life, he knew what those things cost. It was obvious to him that she could not hope to dress as she did or to stay at the Savoy on the salary of a typist. If she worked at all it would be as the whim of a wealthy girl, a very different matter to working as he was compelled to do. Her talk of work to him now seemed shallow and insincere, as if she had said something about going slumming.

On her part, she could do nothing to break through the barrier of reserve that he had set up between them. She tried again, talking about small ships and asking him if he had thought anymore about life at sea. He laughed, a little bitterly. "There's no money in that sort of thing," he replied. "It doesn't get you anywhere. All the work that matters goes on in the office. No, I've done with the sea."

His last words depressed her more than anything. If he could say that he had done with the sea, she felt that he had done with everything she really cared about, deep in her heart. The sea had moulded both of them in adolescence. It had made her practical and self-reliant. It had turned him from a callow suburban schoolboy into a good officer, looked up to by his fellows in the Navy, received by the King at Buckingham Palace and decorated for valour. During the process both had very much disliked the sea with all its hardships, all its crudity and its fatigue, but it had done well for both of them, she knew. Deep in her own mind she knew a debt of gratitude to the sea for all that it had done to mould her. If Donald Wolfe now said that he was done with it, there was indeed a barrier between them. The only thing was, she was pretty sure that he was lying to her again. And there was nothing she could do about it, nothing whatsoever. She had not known him long enough to challenge his sincerity.

She made no more efforts then to break through to the relationship of Portland. She was too proud to go on butting against a brick wall. They talked bright insincerities during the intervals of the show, and they were very flip and smart. He took her to the Dorchester for dinner and they danced a little, but there was no life in it, and about half past eleven she felt that it was late enough for her to say with decency that she had got up frightfully early that morning; that she had been up terribly late every evening that week; that she was just dying on her feet; and did he mind?

He took her back to the Savoy. "This is Maison Porter," she said, with an ineffective attempt at gaiety. "Have one for the road with me." So he allowed her to order a whiskey for him; they drank it in the lounge that overlooks the river, talking in a desultory way about nothing in particular. Behind closed silk curtains a tug hooted suddenly; she glanced quickly at him, and saw his face. He *had* been lying to her; he still cared about the sea.

She tried for the last time. "Funny how that reminds you of things."

He said, "I know. But that's all over and done with now— one can't keep thinking about the war." He seemed to shake himself free of it, and then he glanced at her. "I remember you saying the same thing, about the old soaks in Northampton who lived only for the last war. Major This and Captain That, selling carpet sweepers upon half commission, bragging about all they had done at Ypres twenty years later. One can't go on like that. One's got to forget about the war now, and live in the present."

"I suppose so," she said slowly. "I suppose you're right."

"It's right enough," he said bluntly. "You're not a Leading Wren any more. You're something quite different. And I'm not in command of 1029. I'm something different, too. We may be better or we may be worse, but we're both quite different people."

She said quietly, "Worse, I think. We've both changed a great deal, Donald, in the last six months, and neither of us for the better."

He shrugged his shoulders. "I don't know about that. But anyway, that's the way it is. It's peacetime now. You can't put back the clock."

He got up to go. "It's been terribly good fun this evening," he said brightly. "We must do it again."

She flogged herself to sparkle. "It's been simply wizard. I'll write and let you know when I'm coming down again, and we'll do another show."

They shook hands and said goodnight, still brightly cheerful. He walked out into the winter night with a bitter sense of loss; a thin rain was falling. He could not afford any more taxis and he felt that the walk to the Underground would clear his mind. He turned up his collar and walked on down the glistening pavements. That was the end of that, he thought grimly; it was not very likely that they would ever meet again. If the war had gone on, masking her background, or if her background had been rather more in keeping with his own, they might have become very close friends; they might have loved and married. That would not happen now; there was too much between them. Better to let it go. He thought with a wry smile that one got over things like this. After a time the sharp pain and the sense of loss would fade, and one would think about it as an accident in which one had been hurt a little but in which, by taking the wise course, one had escaped disaster. Better to let it go.

He walked on past Charing Cross and into the park, westward in the rainy night, walking to tire himself and get rid of his trouble. He walked about three miles to Sloane Square station and caught the last train to his suburb. He got home at about two in the morning.

In the Savoy, in the quiet of her air-conditioned room, Jean lay face down on the silk quilt of her bed for a long time, the slow tears running down from her face for the commanding officer who had turned out just another minor businessman. After a time she got up, undressed for bed and took a couple of aspirins. She thought heavily that it was no use going on like that about things. She pulled the curtains and opened the window. It was raining, and the lights shone on the running water of the tideway down below. A faint salty smell came up to her in the luxury of her room. Through all her grief the thought occurred to her that it was fun to have a bedroom looking out over salt water. That took her mind off Donald for a little, and presently she slept.

She was very quiet and thoughtful next morning. She sat in bed eating her breakfast with the window open and her white fur dressing gown around her shoulders; it was a fine, sunny February morning after the rain. From her bed she could see a slice of the river with the barges going up and down, and she sat staring out at them absently.

Donald was over and done with. She knew that it was not now very likely that they would ever meet again. She could not go running after him, pestering him, suggesting other meetings. If he had turned his back upon his naval life, that was his own affair. If that was how he was, she could not change him. But in doing so, she felt that he had turned his back on her. The sea was very dear to her, more dear now that she had been away from it for some months. She would get up presently and ring the bell, and the maid would come and pack her pretty clothes for her, and she would tip the maid and pay her bill and go. She would leave this pleasant room that overlooked the river, leave the faint smell of the sea that drifted up from the tideway, leave the ships and boats behind her, and go home to the Midlands. She found the thought unbearable.

As she sat there in her bed that morning eating toast and marmalade she knew that she had come to one of the turning points in her life. She felt that if she was to be a real person as she had been in the Navy, she must get out of her Northampton groove and get away from home. She did not want to hurt her parents' feelings. She would always go home to them with pleasure for a visit, but their way of life could not be hers. Three years in the Navy had diverted her forever from Northampton. She ached for the old naval life, for the sea, for Donald. She had turned instinctively to Donald, but he had failed her. Naval life was closed to her forever now, but there remained the sea. The sea was always there for anyone who cared to go to it for bitter salt discomfort, fatigue, peril, and peace of mind. She travelled back to Northampton on a lunchtime train, resolved to get away from it as soon as ever she could.

CHAPTER IV

It was a fortnight before she could create an opportunity without hurting her parents by an abrupt departure. In that fortnight she was taciturn and unhappy. She told her parents nothing of what had happened in London, but it was perfectly obvious to them that something had gone wrong with her affairs. She spoke and read a good deal about the sea. It seemed to her parents that she was interested in very little else, and following on this line her father said casually one day, thinking to interest her, "Anthony Clough has heard about his yacht. I saw him at the Club."

Jean looked up quickly. In her present mood anything to do with yachts was interesting to her. "Is that the *Joybelle*?"

"That's the one. She's at St. Peter Port, in Guernsey."

"How did she get there, Daddy?"

"I dunno. She was requisitioned by the Navy. I thought she was sunk at Dunkirk, but apparently that's not right. It seems the Germans salvaged her and used her all the war. He wants to get her back to this country."

Her eyes gleamed. "Daddy, do you think I could go over and help fetch her back?"

Her mother said, "Darling, you don't know what you'd be letting yourself in for."

Jean said, "Oh Mummy, it'd be fun!"

Her parents exchanged glances. It was about the first sign of animation that she had shown since she returned from London, and they were not very anxious to suppress it. Her father

said, "Well, you've met Tony Clough, haven't you? You could
ring him up and have a talk to him about it."

She had met Tony Clough. Tony Clough had been one of
the bright young things of 1920 and was so still in the spirit,
in spite of weighing fifteen stone and twenty-five years in the
boot business. He was a rotund, red-faced little man now, fond
of his beer and a good story. He lived in the country not far
from the Porters and drove down to the office every day. He
was nearly bald and he never took any exercise. Before the war,
he had kept his yacht *Joybelle* in the Hamble river near Southampton, using her as a mobile houseboat for week-ends. He
liked being on the sea but he knew very little about it. On the
few occasions when he had ventured out to sea in the yacht he
had very much disliked the experience. Before the war he used
to move her cautiously about the Solent on very fine days. Ten
miles to Tony was an ocean voyage. His friends said that he
only faced this hazard when his ship began to ground upon
the bottles at low tide. When the war broke out, she had been
requisitioned by the Navy. On her second trip to Dunkirk she
received a near miss from a bomb and drifted sinking towards
the beach with a petty officer dead in her cockpit. There, an
Me.109 found her and spattered her with 20mm shells. That
was the last that had been heard of the *Joybelle* till she turned
up in the Channel Islands after the war.

Jean Porter rang up Tony Clough, and on his invitation she
drove round to have a drink with him. He greeted her jovially,
and poured her out a very large gin and Italian.

"Aye, it's marvellous," he said. "I got the old lady back again
after all these years. I've been through to the Admiralty and
they say she's there, and the Board of Trade, they say I can
have her. I was going to take a run over by air one day next
week and see about getting her fetched back."

Jean said, "Can I come with you, Mr. Clough? I was in
boats all the time I was in the Navy, you know. I'd love to
come and help you bring her home."

He temporised. "Well, I don't know that I was reckoning to bring her home myself, you know. I was thinking I'd find someone over there to sail her back for me."

"How big is she?"

"Forty-seven feet overall."

"Just a nice size for two people to manage. What engines has she got?"

"Two diesels. She does about twelve knots."

Jean said, "Well, what could be nicer than that? We could bring her home ourselves, Mr. Clough—just you and me. Get one other seaman, if you like. But it can't be more than a hundred and twenty miles from St. Peter Port to the Solent. Our M.G.B.'s used to go there and back in a night. It'd only be about ten hours' trip for your boat."

He rubbed his chin. "It's a long way."

She laughed. "It's not. Seriously, Mr. Clough, I'd like most awfully to come and give you a hand with her, if you'll have me. I'll get the willies if I stick around at home much longer."

He glanced at her. "I daresay it takes a bit of getting used to for you girls, settling down after being in the Navy. Well, I was thinking about going Wednesday next."

Jean lived in a dream of anticipation for the next two days. Her first impulse had been to write to Donald and tell him all about it. She restrained herself from that. He had said he was no longer interested in the sea. Later on, perhaps, when this trip to fetch the yacht was over, she could tell him casually about it, to see if she could not revive in him that old enthusiasm for ships which had matched her own when they were in the Navy. But for the time, she felt, she must be patient and not chase him.

When she turned up at the airport to meet Tony Clough she wore her blue serge Wren's skirt and her Wren's white blouse; she had for luggage a naval kitbag full of her boat's crew kit, and she carried a duffle coat. Mr. Clough said, "Look like a proper seaman, you do. I reckon I'd be all right with a crew o' you girls on the yacht, until the missus came to hear of it."

They crossed the Channel by air in the middle of the morning and got to St. Peter Port in time for lunch. They went to the hotel and parked their luggage. After lunch they walked out to the harbour. The *Joybelle* was on a mooring in the middle of the pool; they found a boatman and got rowed out to her. She was not the smart yacht that had stayed very safe in Solent creeks in time of peace. She had been painted grey during the war and her white decks had been tarred; now all this paint and tar was cracking and peeling off, and she was foul with seagull droppings. Below the water line great streamers of seaweed festooned her hull. Several of the windows of her wheelhouse were broken and patched with pieces of cheap plywood, the laminations split and opening. Inside, she was horrible. She stank. A little oily water slopped about the cabin floor, because she had not been pumped out for many weeks. Her mahogany and cedar furnishings had all been daubed over with brown and yellow paint, sick colours that made Mr. Clough feel rising nausea immediately he went below. None of her cushions or crockery were left, her stove and all her kitchen equipment had gone, and she was filthily dirty. Under the engine hatches the machinery looked neglected, and the batteries sulphated and corroded. They tried the lights, but there was no current.

"Oh dear, oh dear," said Mr. Clough sadly. "I dunno that she's worth taking home."

Jean said, "She's a bit of a shambles, but I don't think it's as bad as that, if we can get the engines to go." She looked around her from the wheelhouse. "I'd like to get that Oerlikon mounting off the foredeck; it's right in the view."

"I think I'll sell her as she lies," said Tony Clough, "and get another one built."

"Not for the next five years, you won't," the girl said practically. "There's no building allowed now, and won't be till they've got some houses built in the blitzed areas." She turned to him. "She's yours, and she's the only boat you've got, Mr. Clough, and I'm quite sure if we can get her back to Hamble, Luke's can dish her up just like she was before. And then you'd have a boat with a bit of history behind her."

He brightened at that thought. "Aye," he said. "Have a little bit about her on a brass plate in the wheelhouse, like on passenger steamers that did something in the war."

She smiled, luring him on. "That's right. It'd look fine, that. Not many boats have got a story like she has."

He said, "Well, let's see if we can get this bilge out, for a start."

There was no current in the batteries, so they could not use the electric pump. They found the hand pump and Mr. Clough began to use this; when he had got most of the bilge off the cabin floor, it passed out.

"Sort of choked, or something," he said.

The girl tried it; the handle pulled elastically against her. "There's something bunging up the pipe. Got a dead rat in it, from the feel."

"I'll have to get a man to come and clear it," said Mr. Clough.

"Let's just have a look." Jean stooped down and pulled up the wheelhouse floor hatches; together they traced the pipe from the pump down a bulkhead amongst a lot of other pipes, all stained black and green with oil and verdigris. "There it goes," she said. "It goes down into the well there, between the engines. There ought to be a strainer on the end of it."

Mr. Clough looked with distaste at the black, oily bilge that swirled between the engines as the vessel rolled. "We'll have to get a man to come and see to it," he said again.

"I don't know. It's probably something quite simple." She slipped out of her jacket and rolled up her sleeves, and climbed down in the narrow space between the engines.

Mr. Clough said, "Here, let me do that."

"I'll just see." She plunged her arm down in the black scum and groped about. "God, it's awful stuff!" And then she said, "I've got something here." She reached down further, till her arm was in up to the elbow and the bilge was lapping the rolled sleeve of her white blouse. "There's a strainer here with something soft all around it." She tugged, and brought up a great mass of black, soaked rag, reached down, and brought up another hand full. "Try the pump now, Mr. Clough." He moved the handle, and the black bilge water flowed again into the harbour. Jean climbed up into the wheelhouse and threw the rags over the side. "Hitler's pants," she said scornfully.

Her arm was black with oil up to the elbow, and there were no clean cloths on board. Mr. Clough was rather shocked. "It doesn't matter," she said. "We must get some cotton waste on shore." She wiped her arm on Mr. Clough's handkerchief till it was clean enough to put back in her jacket, and at his suggestion sent the handkerchief to join Hitler's pants.

When they went on shore an hour later the ship was clear of water, and Jean Porter had a streak of black oil under one ear, and her white blouse was completely ruined. They found that there were practically no motor mechanics in the town, and it became clear to them that if they were to get the yacht away in reasonable time they would have to do most of the work themselves.

"Send over to England for a tug or something," Mr. Clough suggested. "Get her towed back to Hamble."

"I don't suppose you'd get anyone to do it," said Jean. "I tell you what. We can get the batteries out of her ourselves and bring them on shore to be charged, and have a go at starting up the engines. If they won't go, then we'll have to see about getting a tow back home."

They found a garage that would charge the batteries. Then they went back to the yacht and in a strenuous hour of work with the assistance of the boatman they got the heavy batteries out of the yacht into the boat, and rowed them on shore. Then they went back to the garage and made them drive a truck down to the quay to fetch the corroded and sulphated cells. The girl would not leave the job till she had seen them in the hands of the electrician and had heard his report on them. Mr. Clough found himself tagging along after her and obeying her instructions. The electrician was noncommittal. He said only that he would empty them out, refill them, put them upon charge, and see what happened.

They went back to the hotel, and Jean Porter had a very necessary bath. She came down to dinner in a clean frock, looking fresh and attractive. Mr. Clough blinked when he saw her, remembering her dealings with the bilge an hour or two before. "Like living with a bloody chameleon," he thought.

After dinner, sitting in the lounge over their coffee, he got out pencil and a notebook and began to jot down a few things they needed to buy. Jean said, "Put down a two-inch Stillson."

"What's that?"

"Big shifting spanner. And we'll want a set of spanners from half inch to one eighth, and a big and a little screwdriver, and a lot of rag or cotton waste, and an oilcan and some oil, and a pot of yellow grease, and some Ouption, and a Primus stove, and a can of paraffin, and some meths." She paused for breath.

He finished writing all this down, and glanced at her curiously. "You like doing this sort of thing, don't you?" he asked curiously.

She smiled. "I suppose I do. It's what I was trained for," she said simply. "Yes, I like it. It's the only sort of job I know." She thought for a minute, and then said, "We'll want a bucket and a scrubbing brush, and a bar of yellow soap."

She came down to breakfast next morning in an old pair of blue serge slacks and a rough blue seaman's jersey, carrying her duffle coat. "I was thinking," she said, "we'd better put down on that list a hank of cod line and about fifteen fathoms of inch and a half rope, and about thirty fathoms of three-inch rope for a warp, if that marine store has any. Manila would be best, but I don't suppose we'll get anything but sisal. And we ought to have a red ensign, too."

Mr. Clough agreed. "Make her look like a yacht."

Jean laughed. "I don't care about that. I was thinking of it as something to hang out upside down if we get into trouble."

They did their shopping in the town, and laden with their purchases they went out again to the yacht. To Mr. Clough's embarrassment and distaste the girl immediately set about cleaning out the lavatory pan and mechanism, which certainly required it, and in decency he had to roll up his sleeves and help her. "You can't be really comfortable in a boat where the heads don't work," she said, and he was compelled to agree with her. And then she laughed. "We can't use the damn thing now," she said. "Put down a roll of paper." He reached for his pencil and his book, wondering what young women were coming to.

They worked on the boat for the rest of the week; at the end of that time she was clean and sweet inside, though still shabby and ugly with the paint and tar that the Germans had slopped on. Looking back upon those days, Mr. Clough was rather surprised to find that he had enjoyed them. The sun had shone most of the time; the harbour water had been blue; and the girl had been so obviously happy in her work. In fact, every minute had been a delight to Jean. Gone were the dull, tiring hours of flogging her brain to be quick in identifying hooks and dashes in the shorthand class, of trying to keep her fingers on the right keys of the typewriter, and of being the worst in her class at both. This boat work was the work she knew and understood and could do well. Tightening a leaky stern gland, or scrubbing the cabin floor, or wiping down the engines with a rag soaked in paraffin, or back splicing the end of a warp, were all occupations of pleasure to her. What the future held for her she did not know, but for the moment she was back where she belonged.

Privately, Mr. Clough rang up her father on the third evening. "Thought I'd just give you a tinkle and let you know Jean's all right," he said. "She's working like a bloody beaver— I've never seen the like of it. You just can't keep her away from the boat. She's out there first thing in the morning, and it's all I can do to get her away in time for dinner at night."

Her father said, "Keeping you on the go, is she?"

"Keeping me on the go?" asked Mr. Clough ruefully, "I'll say she is. I thought I was coming here to get somebody else to sail the boat home for me, but now it seems I've got to sail her home myself. Got me under her thumb properly, she has. We're going to try and get the engines going tomorrow, and if that's all right we might leave about Tuesday or Wednesday. I'm trying to get a fisherman or somebody to come with us as deck hand."

They got the batteries back on board and got the engines running without much difficulty; they moved the ship up to the quay and took on board full tanks of diesel oil and water. They got a pair of mattresses out of an air raid store to furnish her a little, and they bought a few cooking utensils and a little crockery. When all that was done they took the vessel out of the harbour for a trial trip. At full engine revolutions she laboured along at about seven knots instead of the twelve that she had done before the war; her bottom was covered in a growth of thick green weed and long streamers of brown weed trailed behind her. They brought her back and laid her up against a quay wall, and next day paddled round her in gumboots with the boatman scraping and scrubbing the weed off her. They spent the next day buying provisions for the voyage home and searching for a deck hand, which they were quite unable to find. Labour was very short in Guernsey in that first peacetime summer.

Jean said, "It doesn't matter. We can get her across all right between us."

"I'm not much of a sailor," Mr. Clough said doubtfully.

The girl laughed. "I bet she rolls in a beam sea."

They stood in the wheelhouse looking round the yacht, trying to think of anything else that had to be done before they went back to the hotel to pay their bill and fetch their luggage, prepared to start for England next day. There seemed to be nothing else to do; they sat smoking in the wheelhouse together in the afternoon sunshine.

"I don't know what I'd have done without you," Mr. Clough said. "I'd never have been able to tackle all this alone."

"It's been such fun," she said. "I've had a marvellous time. It isn't often that one gets an opportunity like this."

"I don't suppose many girls would feel like that about it," he remarked. "Scrubbing and cleaning out the bilge, and that."

She smiled. "I suppose it's just because it's boats. I wouldn't want to do those jobs at home."

"Not tired of boats, after three years of them in the war?"

She shook her head thoughtfully. "I don't think I'll ever be tired of boats."

He glanced at her. "You'll have to find a young man with a job in boats and marry him," he said, chuckling. "You'll never settle down away from them."

She stared out across the harbour, avoiding his eyes. "There was one once like that," she said, "but he went sour on me."

"Give up coming to see you?" asked Mr. Clough.

"No," she said. "He gave up boats." She glanced at him, and their eyes met, and they both burst out laughing. "Well," said Mr. Clough, "I dunno what to say to that. Were you great friends?"

She said, "We could have been, I think. But it never really got as far as that. It just came to an end."

Mr. Clough felt that if he had been thirty years younger and had had a chance of being great friends with Jean Porter, he would have taken it and stuck to it like glue. Even at the age of fifty-three, she had given him a few disturbing moments, in her close fitting jersey, with the hair blowing across her face. He said decidedly, "He must be a ruddy fool. You're probably well out of it."

"Maybe," she said quietly. "I think we were both ruddy fools, but that's the way things happen."

She did not seem inclined to talk about it any more, and he did not press the subject. They went on shore and got their things from the hotel and heard the weather forecast; it was of a moderate westerly wind with occasional showers. They dined in the hotel and went on board the yacht to sleep, Mr. Clough in the saloon and Jean in the ladies' cabin aft.

She was up at five o'clock in the first light of dawn. Mr. Clough roused to the noise of the Primus stove as she began cooking breakfast. By seven o'clock they had washed up and everything was stowed ready for sea; they started up the engines, dropped the mooring, and steered out of the harbour entrance on their way to England.

They went out northwards through the rocks and hazards of the Little Russell, conning the ship from beacon to beacon with the aid of a small chart of the islands and information upon pilotage that they had gleaned from the boatman. They got through without bumping any rock, and had a brisk argument over the chart as to how to apply magnetic variation to the course, and finally agreed upon a course for the Needles at the west end of the Isle of Wight and steered on it, with a hundred and ten miles to go.

As they cleared the shelter of the land they found a long beam swell in the Channel with a fresh northwesterly wind blowing up a little sea across it. Between the two, The *Joybelle* took up a motion that would have done credit to something at a fun fair. Mr. Clough was steering; he quickly lost his colour and began to lick his lips. Presently he turned to Jean. "Take her for a minute, will you?"

She took the wheel, laughing, and he dived for the wheelhouse door and lost his breakfast over the side. He came back mopping his forehead, white and apologetic, and took the wheel again, but within ten minutes he was at the side again vomiting. After the third spasm she said, "I should go and lie down for a bit. I'll give you a shout if anything happens."

He said forlornly, "Don't you ever get sick?"

"Lord, yes. I don't know why I'm not sick now. It's this stinking cross sea doing it."

She persuaded him to go below, and she stayed at the wheel, steering the course, frowning a little. They were over two hours on their way and she reckoned that they had made good more than twenty miles, but the wind was getting much stronger and spray was flying over the foredeck. The sun had gone in and the weather was grey now, and menacing. Jean held her on course for another hour, a little apprehensive, but enjoying the contest with the elements. So far, apart from the motion, the *Joybelle* was behaving very well.

Soon after ten o'clock the starboard engine slowed. With her heart in her mouth she juggled with the throttle but she could not save it. It idled on irregularly for a minute and then coughed itself to a standstill. Mr. Clough appeared in the hatchway. "What happened?"

"One of the bloody engines died on us," she said. In thought and word she was back in the Navy as a boat's crew Wren. "Can you see if you can get it going while I keep her on course?"

A glance at the compass showed her that while she had been attending to the engine the *Joybelle* had swung round till she was heading somewhere south of east. Jean swung the wheel over, but the ship responded slowly; with the starboard engine out of action and the slower speed the rudder power was insufficient to hold the bow against the wind. The best that she could do was to point about northeast by east and that only with full helm, a course that would take the ship away up Channel.

Beneath her feet she heard the starter groaning, but there was no response. Presently Mr. Clough appeared beside her, white and sick. "I can't get the darned thing to go," he said. "Can't we go on one engine?"

"She won't lie anywhere near the course. Take her for a moment—let me have a go."

She lifted the floor hatch and got down gingerly between the hot engines, one of which was still running. She stared around the mechanism doubtfully. She knew about marine petrol engines and could diagnose a failure in them with some accuracy, but she had never had to do with diesels. Here was no plug to take out to see if it was sparking, here no carburettor needle to tickle to see if fuel was getting through. She took the cap off the service fuel tank, and it was nearly full. The motion of the boat was violent, confusing her; she had too little knowledge and was too bemused to try experiments.

She got up into the wheelhouse again. "I don't know a thing about these engines."

"I don't either. The Skipper always saw to them before the war." He stared at her miserably. "We'd better go back, hadn't we?"

"I think we had." They put the helm over and brought the yacht back on to the reverse course, but now the windage on the other bow prevented a course back to Guernsey; they were heading down towards the maze of reefs and rocks between the Channel Islands and the mainland. "Oh dear," said Mr. Clough unhappily. "What do we do now?"

The girl grinned at him and said, "Have a real good cry." He smiled weakly, and they put the vessel about again to keep away from the land, and studied what course they could lie. "She'll fetch up about Newhaven if we can't do better than this," said Jean. "Maybe the wind'll drop."

She stood at the wheel, and Mr. Clough subsided on the seat behind her, his stomach in turmoil. Jean stood balancing to the motion of the vessel, listening to the steady beat of the one engine that was running, alert for the first sign of faltering. If that one passed out too, she thought, they *would* be in a jam. She was not unduly perturbed about it. Engine failures were nothing new to her as a boat's crew Wren; she was accustomed to the risks that they entailed, and she knew from her experience that everything generally came out all right in the end; alert and competent people did not get drowned in boats. In one sense she was rather pleased that there was incident in this journey; it would be something to write and tell Donald about. She had been longing to write to him, to try and get back their relationship onto something of the old footing; if now they had a passage with a bit of drama in it, as she put it to herself, she could legitimately write to him and tell him all about it. Surely if she did that they would find again the common interests they had when first they met?

As she steered she considered the chart on the chart table beside her. They were doing very little better now than lie straight up the English Channel, much nearer to the coast of France than England; until the wind eased they had little hope of making any headway on their course. It seemed to her that they were doing very little good in going like that. Presently she said, "Ever been to Cherbourg, Mr. Clough?"

He said weakly and without much interest, "No."

"Well, you're going now."

He got up, and she showed him how they stood upon the chart. Cherbourg was straight downwind from them and probably no more than thirty miles away; if the other engine failed they would drift down in that direction anyway, blown by the wind. It was obviously sensible to make for it. They put the vessel on an estimated course for Cherbourg and went on, hoping that the one remaining engine would keep turning till they got there.

They had no sailing directions for the port, and knew nothing of it beyond its location on their small-scale chart. "I expect it'll be pretty obvious when we get there," Jean said cheerfully. It was more to write about to Donald. "If not, we'll put her on a beach somewhere and get out and walk."

The prospect of near-shipwreck did not appeal to Mr. Clough. "Sooner the better," he said feelingly.

They sighted a large island over to the starboard presently, which Jean identified as Alderney. Thereafter, they had little difficulty. They picked up Cap de la Hague and followed the coast round at a safe distance from the miles of jagged reefs that ran out from it, till in the early afternoon a great manmade breakwater appeared with a wide entrance facing them. They steamed through it to the Grand Rade de Cherbourg, hoping it was free from mines and other nastiness. A small motor boat full of American soldiers showed them the way into the Avant Port, and they berthed alongside a raft of N.L. pontoons in the middle of the town. They were rather shocked at the sight of the many sunken ships still lying in the harbour and at the devastation of the quays and docks; a seaport that has been fought over as Cherbourg was is a sad sight.

For a while they sat resting in the wheelhouse, smoking cigarettes and looking at the town, recovering their emotional poise after the anxieties of the day, while a few Frenchmen in black berets and small boys in smocks stood looking at them from the raft. Then they went below and washed and had a meal, and after that they walked ashore together to the office of the Douane. They had no passports or ship's papers, but that did not seem to mean a great deal to the Frenchmen. So much had happened to them there in Cherbourg that they had grown tolerant of small irregularities.

Returning to the yacht, they stopped and gossiped with the crew of an American Army launch moored to the same raft ahead of them. One of the Americans said, "I'd say you got a filter blocked. That's the only thing that ever stops a Diesel on all cylinders at once."

A lanky young man picked up a kit of tools and strolled over to the yacht with them, and in ten minutes had extracted a cup full of sand and textile fluff from one filter and half a cup full from the other. He showed Jean what to do if it happened again, and waited while they started up the erring engine. "Guess you won't get no more trouble with that now," he said, and lounged away again, embarrassed by their thanks.

They dined on shore in the main hotel, came back early to the yacht, full of good French food and wine, and went to bed. They made an early start next day from Cherbourg and crossed to England without incident except that Mr. Clough was sick again. They left at seven in the morning, sighted the Isle of Wight at about noon, and steamed up the Hamble river to Luke's Yard at about five in the afternoon.

As the motors came to rest, Mr. Clough said, "Now I'm going to confess to something. I've been a ruddy fool, I have. Do you know, I hadn't got a penny of insurance cover on her? If anything had happened, the ship wasn't covered at all."

Jean said, "Well, nothing did happen. If you'd insured her, you'd have spent the premiums for nothing."

"That's not the way to look at it at all," said Mr. Clough. "That's the way to bankruptcy, that is. I'll have to see about it now." He reflected for a minute. "The broker that I used to go to for marine work, he died in the war. Got bombed in his house, he did. I'll have to look around and find another."

Jean's heart leaped. It was too easy. "I know a chap who works for a marine insurance broker in the City," she said casually. "Minchin and Bowater. I could ask him to get in touch with you, if you like." Now that the strain of the passage was over she was longing to tell Donald all about it, to tell him because he would understand what had been involved, because he would tell her that she had done well. Though he had said that he was finished with the sea, surely Donald would be interested in this? It wouldn't be chasing him, surely, if she was to suggest that they meet again so that she could tell him all about it? And this insurance for the *Joybelle* would be the excuse.

"I've heard of Minchin and Bowater," said Mr. Clough.

"They'd do as well as anyone. Tell him to give me a ring back at the office."

They went on shore to the Bugle for a drink and dinner. Over the meal Jean said diffidently, "I don't believe you'll get much work done on the *Joybelle*, Mr. Clough, unless you have somebody down here sitting on the job for you. There's too much competition for the men." She hesitated. "How would you feel about it if I was to stay on down here for a bit and get the yard going on the work you want done?"

He cocked an eye at her. "Don't your father and mother want you at home?"

"They do. But I'd much rather stay on down here for a bit."

"Not much for you in Northampton, is there?"

"No," she said, "there's not. It's a frightful pity, but I don't think I could ever settle down up there. I've been messing about with boats now for so long I've kind of got into the way of it. If it would help you if I stay on down here chasing up the yard and working on the boat a bit myself, that's what I'd like."

He was sorry for her. He was no fool, and he could understand the rather pathetic groping after a new way of life that she had displayed to him. The job on the *Joybelle* would not last her more than a few weeks and after that she would have to do something different, but he would not deny her that short time of mental ease. "Suits me," he said briefly.

He placed his order for the reconditioning of the *Joybelle* with the yard next day and went off in a taxi to Southampton on his way back to his Midland office. When he was gone, Jean went to a call box in the village and rang up Minchin and Bowater in London. When a man answered, she asked, "May I speak to Mr. Wolfe, please?"

He answered her. "Mr. Wolfe isn't with us any longer."

She was astonished. "Not with you? When did he leave?"

"About a week ago."

"Do you know where he's gone to—where I can telephone him?"

"I don't think you'll be able to do that," the man said. "I understand he's left the country. He told us he was going to Newfoundland."

She said something or other and hung up, and stood in the stuffy little call box staring at the doodles on the wall, hurt and lost, and full of pain. This was the end of it, the final and irrevocable end. In years to come when time had eased the sharp grief that had come upon her now, there might be other men, but she knew that there would never be another man like Donald.

CHAPTER V

Many men turn the corner of their lives while drinking at a bar, and it was at the bar of the R.N.V.R. club in London in that first postwar spring that Donald Wolfe turned his. Six months in the insurance business in the City, after six years at sea in motor torpedo boats, had sickened him of office life. Like most men, he would have stuck to it if there had been a young woman in the offing, if he had had the incentive of marriage ahead of him, or even of a good deal of money. In Minchin and Bowater there was no great money lure to keep him on his office stool, and since his evening at the Savoy Hotel with Leading Wren Jean Porter, he was sour and bitter about what had receded far beyond his reach. Naturally, he turned to gin and good company at his club in the evenings. He was already slippery upon his office stool. It was at the bar that he received the final push that toppled him off it.

Freddie Sparkes gave him the push. Freddie was a man of many interests and some means, and an old acquaintance of Donald from the days when they had both been sub-lieutenants in the early motor gunboats. He came into the bar where Donald was sitting morose with an evening paper and said, "Bought a boat today."

Donald raised his head. "What kind of a boat?"

The other laughed shortly. "Pig in a poke, old boy. A twenty-five ton yacht, named *Kittiwake*." He pulled out his wallet and extracted from it a Kodak print of a yawl lying in a barren, stony inlet of the sea. "That's about all I know about her."

Donald Wolfe studied the print. "Looks all right. Where is she now?"

"There, that's where she is." He indicated the photograph. "That's a place called Twillingate in the northeast coast of Newfoundland. It's an island, I believe. The chap who owned her left her there when war broke out. Sixty miles from railhead, old boy, by sea in the summer or by dog sled over the ice in the winter. I tell you, this is He-Man stuff, this is."

Wolfe stared at him. "Do you mean you bought her without seeing her?"

"That's right. I got her for a hundred quid."

The *Kittiwake* had been built in Newfoundland by an English yachtsman who had cruised the coast in her before the war, and left her at Twillingate when war broke out. He had come home to join the Navy, and had died in a corvette in the North Atlantic in 1942. In winding up his estate the executors had puzzled over what to do with a yacht at Twillingate. She had stayed on their hands for four years until Freddie, who would take a flyer in any kind of business, and who was a second cousin of the widow, offered a hundred pounds for the vessel as she lay. The executors had jumped at the offer, and had promptly sealed the bargain with a letter. She was now Freddie's property and he, in turn, was wondering what to do about her.

"She'd sell all right if I could get her over here," he said. "Yachts are going for the most fantastic prices. Get a thousand for her in this country, easily." He scrutinised the photograph. "She looks all right there, doesn't she?"

"That was taken seven years ago," said Donald.

"That's true enough. She's probably a perfect wreck by now. I'll have to get somebody to go out there and look her over, I suppose. If she's any good, she'll have to be got down to St. John's and shipped back here, deck cargo on a freighter. Do her up and use her myself for a bit, perhaps."

Donald said quietly, "Who would you get to do that for you?"

"I dunno. Everybody seems to be working, that's the trouble. Except the ones you wouldn't trust out of your sight. Do you know anyone who'd go and do a job like that?"

"Yes," replied Donald. "I would."

The decision was made as easily as that. "I don't want to pay much," Freddie Sparkes said cautiously. "I thought, pay all expenses, of course, and about fifty quid for the trouble."

Donald said, "I'd go for that. I'm just about through with the bloody office."

When he got home that evening, having clinched the deal with Mr. Sparkes, he was quite certain he had made the right decision. He remained certain of it even after the reproaches from his father next day.

"It's no good, Dad," he said. "I've given the insurance business a good tryout, and I don't like it. Now I'm going to poke around and see if I can't find a job I do like. This is a first shot."

His mother wailed, "But Donald dear, there doesn't seem to be any future in it. You said yourself that this is only going to last for two or three months."

"I know," he said cheerfully. "After that I'll have to poke around and find another job."

He sailed for St. John's ten days later. On arrival there, he set himself to find his way to Twillingate. As the train northwards and across the island ran only twice weekly, he had to stay for a couple of days in the shabby, wooden capital. That gave him an opportunity to adjust himself to the atmosphere of hardship in the place. He left by train at the end of the week for Notre Dame junction and for Lewisport, where he waited for another two days for a boat for Twillingate, amongst the islands off the east coast.

It was a late season, and the sea was still full of small pack

ice when he left Lewisport on the last stage of his journey. He
went in a motor boat that plied among the islands, laden with
crates and bales of stores, and a few passengers. There was a
local trader and his family returning from their annual holiday
among the twenty-odd houses of Lewisport, and a couple of
fishermen returning from a winter job on shore. The trader
was a thoughtful, slow-spoken man named Mitchison. He knew
all about the *Kittiwake*. "She's been lying up at Marshall's Landing all the war," he said. "Joe Clements has been looking after
her, pumping her out, and that. Looked after her as though
she was his baby, the whole six years. If you've come to fetch
her away, mister, I reckon you or somebody owes Joe a packet
for what he done all those years."

At Twillingate, Donald Wolfe was glad to accept an invitation to stay with the Mitchisons for the night in their rambling
wooden shack that was the trader's store at one end and a small
farm at the other. He hired a motor boat next day to take him
to Marshall's Landing seven miles away. This turned out to be
a narrow, stony creek, well sheltered from the winter gales. As
it opened out before him, Donald saw two small wooden shacks
upon the barren shore and three small sailing vessels anchored
off. There was nothing else there but the bare hill sweeping up
to the skyline. He recognised one of the ships at once as the
yacht that had appeared in Freddie's photograph, back in distant London. As they drew near, he saw that she was practically
devoid of paint, her colour the greyish white of bare, weath-
ered wood.

Half an hour later he was on board her, talking to Joe
Clements. Mr. Clements was a fisherman who was now too
old for fishing on the Newfoundland Banks. He was a shabby
old man dressed in a dirty blue jersey and pants made out of
sailcloth. He lived in one of the shacks on the shore with his
wife, as old and shabby and dirty as he was. The so-called
yacht was very roughly finished, built of local timber on a

beach at Twillingate in 1938, iron fastened, and massively con-
structed. She had been left with Mr. Clements at the beginning
of the war and, at first, he had received regular payments for
her maintenance from the owner. Presently he heard of the
owner's death, and no more payments came. In 1943, he had
received a letter from the executors, and had got Mitchison to
answer it for him, being unable to write himself. He had put
this letter away carefully with his wife's marriage lines and one
or two similar documents that were evidently important and
not very clearly understood. He had continued to care for the
yacht because caring for ships was his whole life. Nobody had
paid him any money and he had asked for none since 1942.

"Pretty good shape she's in, considering," the old man said.
"I laid her ashore there on the beach two years back, 'n hard-
ened down the caulking, 'n she don't leak none. I dunno about
the motor. Dwight Mitchison, he said to fill the cylinders with
oil, and I done that each year. I got her sails up at the house, in
the loft."

Donald looked around him. There was little paint left on
the ship; the masts stood stark and bare, the standing wire
corroded and rotten. He had expected nothing better. Seven
years would of necessity leave their mark upon a ship that was
laid up. Apart from that, she had been cared for well; the deck
seams were freshly caulked, and inside she was clean and dry.
"I think you've done a darned good job," he said.

He spent an hour on the ship with Mr. Clements, and another hour in the loft of his shack on shore turning over and
examining the sails and rope rigging. After that, Mr. Clements
took him down into the frowsiness of the shack for an unpleasant and rather dirty mug of tea, and they settled the sum
that should be paid to the old man for all his years of work.
From that, over a cigarette, they drifted into a discussion of
the future.

"I guess I'll leave this place and go to Cornerbrook," the

old man said. His trust was completed now, and he could go. "I got a married daughter there, 'n there's good money to be picked up making barrels for the herring fishers on the east coast. That's all an old chap like me can do now, just making barrels."

They stood together in the doorway of the shack looking out over the rocky, barren creek. "You'll see a bit more of life there," said Donald.

"Aye, Cornerbrook's a fine big place. I did hear they've got a movie theatre there." He turned, and said over his shoulder, "Guess you'll like that, Ma."

"Aye," she said, "that's right." Throughout his dealings with the Clements family, Donald never heard the wife say anything else.

He blew a cloud of smoke, thoughtfully. "Who do those other boats belong to?" He indicated the two fishing vessels anchored by the yacht.

"One of 'em's mine," the old man said. "The one this side— *Mary*, I call her, after Ma. The other one belongs to Stan Higgins."

Donald stood looking at the ships. The *Mary* was not unattractive in her lines; she was heavily built, cutter rigged, and with the fine sheer of a Banks schooner; she was about forty feet in length. "What'll you do with the *Mary*?" he asked. "Sell her?"

"Maybe, if I got an offer."

Donald Wolfe said slowly, "Well, I might make an offer for her, if she's sound."

It was not a snap decision on his part. It was the crystallisation of an idea that had been in the back of his mind for some time. If the market in yachts in England was so good that Freddie Sparkes could afford to buy a pig in a poke and bring it home to sell, it might be possible for Donald Wolfe to do the same. At home, he knew, no yachts were being built and everybody seemed to be demanding them. Prices were rocketing up. Almost any sort of craft was saleable, and would be for some time.

"She's sound enough," the old man said. "Fifteen year old she is, 'n not a patch of rot in her anyplace. If they don't rot in the first seven year, they won't rot ever. And fastenings as good as when they was put in."

They got into the motor boat again, and went out to the *Mary*. She had a small cabin or cuddy aft, with the centre portion of the ship given over to a hold or fish well, in the bottom of which lay the stone slabs of ballast. The sails and running gear were good. She was a sturdy, roomy vessel, probably rather slow, but a ship that could go anywhere.

"I'd like to see her out of the water," Donald said at last. "If you sold her, Mr. Clements, what would you want for her?"

The old man said, "Would seven hundred dollars be too much, mister?"

Donald Wolfe went back that evening in the motor boat to Mitchisons at Twillingate, wrote out a long cable about the *Kittiwake* to Freddie Sparkes, and put it in with the mail leaving on the boat for Lewisport next day. That was his duty, but his mind was full of the *Mary*; he had resolved to buy her for himself. The queer thought came to him that he would like to sit down and write to Jean Porter and tell her all about the *Mary*. Surely, even in her new life as a wealthy girl, she would be interested in a thing like this? He thought a little grimly that, if he bought the *Mary*, by the time he got her home, he wouldn't have enough money left to buy Jean Porter a bun in a tea shop, let alone a dinner at the Dorchester, the sort of entertainment that she seemed to expect. It was better not to start all that again, at any rate until he could afford to take her out. Better to let it rest. He did not write.

The next day he went back to Marshall's Landing, taking his bedding with him. He had fallen into the way of the country by that time. He travelled with his blankets and a little food, prepared to live anyhow or anywhere. At Marshall's Landing he stayed with the Clements, sleeping in the frowsy stuffiness of the shack upon a mattress laid upon the floor before the kitchen fire.

They put the *Mary* on the beach next morning for an examination of the hull, leaning her up against a great flat-sided rock at high water and waiting till the tide left her. Donald walked around her, prodding with a knife in search of soft spots in the planking, but he could find nothing wrong. They floated her off again in the late afternoon, and that evening in the shack he bought her, paying over the seven hundred dollars in notes.

"What are you going to do with her, now you've got her?" the old man asked.

Donald said, "I want to get her home. I don't know how much the shipping would cost, yet."

"Deck cargo—along with the *Kittiwake*?"

"That's right."

There was a long silence. "Cost more 'n you've paid for her," the old man said at last. "They're telling me that rates for shipping anything are mighty high these days."

"What would you think of sailing her home?"

"To England? You mean, just by yourself?"

"I think so."

"It's a mighty long way."

"Fifteen hundred and fifty miles, to Ireland."

The old man sucked his pipe. "She'd do it all right, but could you?"

Donald laughed awkwardly. "I don't know. I've been at sea as long as that before. Say three weeks."

"Aye, but in a big ship."

"Yes. In a destroyer."

"You've got other folks to share the work in a big ship," the old man said. He spat into the grate. "You'll likely get the wind behind you all the way," he said. "I reckon if you're going to sail her home, you'd want to make a square sail. Dwight

Mitchison, he's got some medium weight cloth that would do."

He went out onto the hill behind his shack next morning and fetched down a sapling that had been cut the year before, and set to work to trim it into a yard for the square sail. Donald Wolfe went into Twillingate and bought the sailcloth, and together they set to work with palm and needle to sew up the long lengths of the seams by hand. "It don't take long, when you know how," the old man said. He was shipwright and sailmaker and fisherman together, and had been so all his life.

A few days later they received a cable from Freddie Sparkes, authorising Donald to go ahead and ship the *Kittiwake* to England. He had to break off work on the *Mary* then, and make arrangements for the yacht to be towed down to St. John's by the weekly passenger boat. He went down with the tow, and stayed three weeks in the capital, until at last he saw the yacht resting on a cradle on the deck of the freighter, leaving the quayside for England.

He got back to Twillingate about the middle of May. By that time the weather was fine and the days long, and there was no more pack ice in the sea. He found the *Mary* very nearly ready for sea. Joe Clements had been working on her busily while he had been away. The old man had a great affection for his boat. He had helped to build her many years before, and he had used her and cared for her throughout the latter part of his life. Now he was parting with her, but the wrench was mitigated for him by the fact that she was going to sail the Atlantic, a long fine voyage, and a fit departure for the good boat he had loved. While Wolfe had been away, he had worked on her from dawn till dusk. He had scraped and tarred her bottom, painted the topsides and the deck, and overhauled the running gear. He showed Donald the expenses that he had incurred at Mitchison's to fit her for the voyage, but he would take no payment for his work.

"That's nothin'," he said shortly. "I wouldn't want to see her go away on a long trip like that 'less she was all squared off to go."

In his three weeks at St. John's, Donald Wolfe had become determined to sail the vessel home, and to sail her home alone. He had no illusions about the hazards of the voyage. He knew that three weeks single-handed in the North Atlantic would be both dangerous and exhausting; if things went wrong he might well lose his life. That was a gamble that he had to take, if he was to make sufficient money out of the *Mary* to keep him for a time while he looked around for something else to do. The purchase of the ship had run his finances dangerously low. If she were to be shipped to England as deck cargo, it was doubtful that he would have any money left at all when he got back. By sailing her home, he would save the cost of shipping her, and there would be a credit, too. The sixty pounds or so that his return passage would have cost Freddie Sparkes would be due to him. In that way he would still have well over a hundred and fifty pounds left to draw upon when he got back to England, and he would have the *Mary* to sell. He would be several pounds the richer when the ship was sold, with sufficient money to keep him without working for a year while he looked round for more congenial work than the insurance office.

He dallied for a few days with the idea of hiring some fisherman to sail with him, but the cost of the man's wage and the cost of his passage back to Newfoundland deterred him. If he could sleep with some certainty upon the voyage, he felt that there was no reason why he should not make the trip alone. It had been done before, and it was summer weather.

He talked over the problem of sleeping with Joe Clements. "You'll sleep all right if she's hove to," the old man said. "I done that many a time. But under way—well, I dunno. Maybe with that square sail set 'n the main down she'd hold her course for you. I guess you'll have to try it out and see."

They tried it as they sailed her down together to St. John's for loading up with stores before departure. Sailing with the square sail and the helm lashed, the ship was more or less stable on her course; she yawed about a good deal, but she did not run wild or get out of control. It was clear from their tests that it would be possible to go below and sleep while the wind was aft and while the weather remained fair. In bad weather it would be necessary to set the mainsail and heave to in order to sleep.

At St. John's, he spent a drunken evening with Joe Cements, and took him to the station next day and put him on the train for Lewisport. They said good bye. "It's been real nice to know you," the old man said. His fuddled mind drifted back to his ship. "You treat her right and she'll treat you all right," he said. "She never let me down."

Donald said, "I'll write and tell you how I get on."

"Aye, write a letter. The wife, she reads fine."

The train steamed off up the single track, and Donald began his shopping in St. John's. He bought a hundred gallon galvanised iron water tank and installed it in the hold. He bought a side of bacon and a small sack of flour and a large number of tinned foods, sufficient for sixty days at sea. He did not cater for a very varied diet, for he would have little time for cooking. Bacon, corned beef, beans, biscuit, and sweet tea were to be his staple foods. He aimed no higher than that.

In St. John's, he managed to buy a second-hand sextant and a nautical almanac. As he had no reliable watch or chronometer, he would have to navigate by latitude alone. His navigation plan was simple. The nearest point of the British Isles to Newfoundland was the west coast of Ireland. To reduce the risk of missing it by faulty navigation, he would set his course for Galway, in the middle. He planned to steer a northeast course until he got upon the latitude of Galway about the tenth day out; thereafter he would sail along that latitude until he got there, guessing at the distance run each day.

He sailed at dawn one morning at the end of May. It would be idle to pretend that he was not frightened. In spite of his long war experience at sea, he was very nearly sick with fright when he sailed alone out of St. John's with over eighteen hundred miles of sea ahead of him. It was a grey morning with a moderate southwesterly wind, a fair wind for his purpose. He set his square sail and settled down to blow before it. In a few hours, the land had faded behind him and there was nothing but a grey, rough, inhuman sea around him and ahead.

He left the helm after a time and went down into the cuddy to make a cup of tea upon his Primus stove to steady his nerves. Moreover, it was better to know the worst about the ship sailing herself before he got too far away from land. He came up on deck a quarter of an hour later with his mug of tea, a little surprised to find that everything was still all right. The deck was just as he had left it, the ship rolling and labouring across the swell. He drank his tea more confidently, and busied himself about the deck with a succession of little jobs.

Donald spent some time during that first day in perfecting his system of navigation, and this kept his mind occupied. The ship was forty feet long, not counting the bowsprit; a calculation showed him that at a speed of four knots a piece of paper or a wisp of old rope dropped over the bow would reach the stern in ten seconds. He spent a good deal of the first day in dropping things over the bow and running quickly to the stern to time them, watch in hand. As he gained experience he found that he could gauge the speed by eye with some accuracy, but he used this method as a check throughout the voyage.

He entered his speed every two hours in a notebook, and from this he calculated the distance run each day and marked off his position on the chart. That first day was grey and overcast and he could take no sights; when he took his first sight for latitude two days later it showed him to be thirty miles north of his dead reckoning position. He spent some time agonising over this discrepancy, and finally put down his guessed position on the chart half way between the two. Later he came to have more confidence in his observations as successive sights confirmed the first.

For the first two days, he was beset with fear. Fear haunted him, wherever he went, whatever he did. While he was sitting at the helm throughout the long, slow hours he was afraid the ship might start a plank through some defective fastening, let in a great rush of water to the hold, fill, and sink. He watched every tremor of the mast uneasily, fearful that it was working too much, that the backstays would not hold it, that it would carry away and break and crash down into the sea beside the ship. Watching the compass card and the grey horizon, he was beset with fears that he had made a mistake in navigation, that something was wrong with the position of the sun, that they were going the wrong way across the unmarked waste of sea. In his short trips below to cook food he was terrified that he would find the ship in trouble when he went on deck again. That she never was did not assuage his fears. Each time the rudder clunked and grumbled, which it did with every wave, he feared that something must be wrong with the pintles down below the water line, that it would jam, and presently come off and float away, and leave the vessel uncontrollable to broach to in the waves, swamp, and sink.

Always before when he had been to sea there had been other men about him who were more frightened than he; that very fact had kept him free from fear. He knew these fears were quite unreasonable, but he could not rid himself of them. When evening came, that first grey evening in the Atlantic, they grew upon him till he was close on panic. He had made every preparation for the ship to sail herself during the night, but for a long time he could not force himself to go below. Finally, realising that the surest way to accident was through his own fatigue, he went down to his bunk, resolved to lie in it till two o'clock in the morning.

He did not sleep at all, but lay awake, glancing at his watch now and then, thinking what a fool he was not to be able to sleep, listening to all the noises of the vessel, terrified that some of them were dangerous. At two in the morning he released himself and went on deck. He found everything in order, because he had done his work well in the evening and the wind had not increased. He gauged the speed as well as he could in the darkness and wrote it in his book. Then he made himself a cup of tea and lay down again, determined not to get out of his bunk till six.

He dozed a little then between his bouts of fear. The sense of loneliness was heavy on him, and in his short spells of uneasy sleep, he dreamed. He dreamed that he was sailing the *Mary* into a small harbour and bringing her alongside a quay, and Jean Porter was there dressed in her Wren's clothes, the rough serge trousers and the seaman's jersey that showed her figure so pleasantly. She was standing on the quay and smiling at him. She said, "If you'll chuck me a warp, sir, I'll make it fast on this bollard."

He turned over and woke up in disappointment and loneliness and fear, because Jean Porter would never be a Wren again. She had turned into something totally different and no good to him, up in Northampton where the boots were made, and he was alone and afraid in the middle of the Atlantic in an old sailing boat. Presently he drifted into an uneasy sleep again, and he was bringing the *Mary* into a calm anchorage between wooded hills, and Jean Porter was there in the L.C.P. that she had driven at Portland when they first met. She said, "There's a mooring buoy just up the harbour, sir. You'll be all right there. If you'll take my line I'll give you a tow up to it." He rolled over and woke again, in disappointment and loneliness.

When he went on deck at six o'clock the sun was up, the wind had dropped a little and the clouds were clearing off. With the sunshine, some of his fears were assuaged. He was feeling weak and ill through lack of sleep and strain, but he ate a good breakfast and felt better. The ship was running easily now at about three and a half knots; he trimmed the square sail sheets and set the helm again, and presently he went below and lay down on his bunk and slept more quietly for an hour or two.

He settled down into a routine after that, and gradually his fears left him. It was some days before he could sleep quietly at night, and he had recurrent dreams of being rescued by Jean Porter in her motor boat. But as the days went on he found that he could sleep more restfully each night, and that it was possible to think of the future and pleasant things while sitting at the helm.

For the first half of his crossing the weather was kind to him and the ship behaved well. Each day brought a moderate westerly wind that carried him along towards Ireland. His worst day's run was about seventy miles and his best a hundred and twelve. By his dead reckoning of distance run he passed longitude 31 degrees west on the evening of the tenth day; this he calculated to be the half way point of his crossing. He celebrated it with a tinned plum pudding garnished with his medicinal brandy.

On the morning of the twelfth day, the barometer began to drop. He watched it uneasily as the day went on. It fell two points in five hours, and at the same time the wind backed to the south and began to rise. It was evident that there was a depression coming up behind him. He could no longer lie his course under the square sail. He took it in, and set the mainsail well reefed down, and a small storm jib.

The next two days were sheer, unmitigated hell. The wind increased till it was blowing at full gale force from the southeast. The sea got up and the wind blew the crests off the waves and over the ship continuously. It rained heavily and horizontally, so that the air was full of flying water. He stayed anxiously at the helm, and became soaked to the skin in a very short time in spite of oilskins and sea boots. He remained in the same wet clothes for the rest of the gale. As night came on it

grew very cold, and he became numb and mentally slow on
this account. He tried to combat the cold with a hot drink,
but the wind had brought up a steep new run of seas across
the long westerly swell, so that the motion of the boat was
irregular and violent. He could not stand to hold a saucepan
on his stove to cook a hot drink. In his efforts to do so he fell,
spilled the cocoa from the pan, scalded his hand painfully, and
got no cocoa.

He became afflicted with a sort of stupor due to cold and
nausea. He was not actually sick at that time, being a good
sailor, but he became very listless and slow, and disinclined to
try to eat anything. His mind worked sluggishly, and new im-
pressions took a long time to register. He hove the ship to at
nightfall, but stayed at the helm. As the centre of the depression drew nearer, the wind increased. By two in the morning,
the ship would not lie hove to any longer. She began to fall off
from the wind in the trough of the seas, wallowing. Then she
would come up to the wind again with all sails shaking with
insensate violence, and then fall off again. It took him a quarter of an hour to appreciate the trouble, while the sails flogged
above him and his chilled, dulled brain turned over slowly in
the racket.

When at last he took action he crawled forward to the mast
and eased both peak and main halyards a little to lower the
boom down onto the deck. At great risk of injury, working in
the dark, he managed to get a line round it and lash it down
on the quarter. He crawled forward to the mast again and lowered away both halyards and got the gaff down to the deck. In
attempting to control that in the insensate rolling of the ship,
he received a violent blow from it upon the shoulder and neck,
and a minute later his left hand was crushed between the flying spar and the boom as he tried to get a line round it. Weeping
with pain, for there was nobody to see and it seemed to make
the pain easier to weep, he got the gaff secured at last. He
crept forward again and slacked away the jib halyard, lowered

the jib into the sea, and pulled it on board with the greatest difficulty due to the violent motion of the vessel and his injuries. Then he went back to the helm, and settled down dully, a mass of pain, to steer the ship downwind.

She ran fairly easily under bare poles, but the motion was intense. He was sick now in real earnest, partly due to shock from the pain of his hand and his shoulder. He vomited repeatedly over the side of the cockpit onto the seaswept deck. After a while the vomiting ceased and he sat on in stupor at the helm as the grey dawn came up under leaden clouds. He swayed loosely to the motion of the vessel in intense fatigue, as the rain slashed at him horizontally. Once or twice that day, he stirred himself and tried to eat and drink something, but instantly vomited again. He may have dozed a little at the helm, for night came again before he was ready for it, and he sat on at the tiller, chilled, torpid, only half alive. So thirty-six hours passed, and the *Mary* drove on over the Atlantic northwards in the direction of Iceland, making about three knots before the gale.

On the evening of the second day the wind decreased and began to work round to the west again. Donald Wolfe was past caring much by that time. He had found by experiment that nothing much happened if he left the tiller; the windage of the mast was forward of the centre of lateral resistance of the hull, and when under no control she lay with the seas upon her quarter, running more or less downwind. As the wind moderated he left the deck and went below and shut the hatch down after him and fell upon his bunk still in his wet oilskins and sea boots, and presently a little warmth crept back into his body, and he slept.

When he awoke three hours later, the wind had dropped to a fresh breeze and the night was cloudless and starry. He put his head out of the hatch and looked around. The ship seemed to be all right, so he went below again. He managed to make himself a cup of Bovril then and to eat a biscuit, and by lying down again at once, he retained them. He slept again, and when he woke it was full daylight. There was sunshine out on deck, and only a light breeze.

He did not hurry about getting under way, but cooked himself a meal and pumped the water out of the bilges. Presently, he went out on deck and crept around to inspect the damage caused by the gale, and found nothing wrong at all. Not one rope's end was chafed or parted; not one sail was torn. The ship was one hundred percent in order. All the damage was confined to his own body. All the danger had lain in his own weakness. As always, the ship had been stronger than the man.

With great difficulty and pain from his injuries, he got the mainsail hoisted again, and then the jib and foresail. He got the vessel on a course and hove to for a sight at noon, which showed the vessel to have been blown about a hundred and ten miles to the north. He made the necessary correction to the course and went on. That night he hove to for the hours of darkness, had a large meal, and slept fairly quietly all night.

Seven days later he began to see seabirds in large numbers, and judged that he was getting near to land. He hove to again that night and went on at dawn. About the middle of the forenoon, land appeared ahead of him, a faint blue line of mountains on the far horizon. That evening he sailed into a sea loch called Kilkieran Bay, and dropped his anchor in a sandy little cove without a house in sight, twenty-four days out from St. John's.

CHAPTER VI

During the months since Jean Porter had returned from Guernsey with the *Joybelle*, she had been living at Hamble, the chief
yachting port on the south coast of England. She had settled
down there very comfortably, living in the *Joybelle* in the shipyard, cooking her own food, with occasional meals on shore at
the local public house, the Bugle. She wore serge trousers,
stained and dirty, and much of her Wren clothing. She spent
half her time badgering the shipyard to put more men onto
the reconditioning of the yacht, and the other half in getting
on with some of the scraping and painting herself. And on the
whole, she was happy.

She would have been happier if she had not been dithering
between two different modes of life. Like most normal girls,
she liked pretty clothes and beauty parlours, and flowers, and
parties and theatres. She got none of those at Hamble, where
her daily round was utterly remote from the life she had led at
her home in Northampton. That life had not brought her any
great contentment. Indeed, she was vaguely aware that it had
lost Donald for her. This life that she was leading at Hamble
was satisfying to one part of her because it meant that she was
busy all day long in work that she could do and do quite well.
Three years in the Navy as a boat's crew Wren had taught her a
good deal about painting and varnishing and overhauling boats.
Having to choose between the work she knew and liked, or
life in Northampton sitting about in pretty clothes waiting for
somebody—not Donald—to marry her, she chose Hamble.
But there were times when she was sorry about the clothes,

and utterly fed up with cooking her own meals alone over a Primus stove in a vessel covered with wet paint.

Most of the friends that she made at Hamble in that first postwar summer were girls like herself. Hamble was full of ex-Wrens at that time. Jean Porter was not the only girl who had found after the war that there was little that she cared for in her home, and who had turned back to the sea. Some of these girls were old friends who had been in the boats with her in the Navy. They turned up one by one at Hamble on some boat or other, dressed in their old serge trousers and their summer flannels, seeking the life that they had known and found satisfying. They congregated there on various pretexts, finding little jobs to do up and down the river with the yachts, as badly adjusted as she was to the life of peace, tactfully avoiding the monotony of home.

Deborah Curtis, late of *H.M.S. Mastodon,* came to Jean one sunny afternoon as she was varnishing the wheelhouse. She said, "Want a run down the river? Sam Little says he's got to send his launch down to tow a yacht in." Sam was the foreman of the yard. "He hasn't got a man to spare, so I said I'd go for him."

Jean laid down her brush. "Okay. When is it?"

"Now. She's anchored somewhere off the Spit buoy."

"Hasn't she got an engine?"

"I suppose not."

"What sort of yacht is it?"

"I dunno. Sam said she's come over from America. The owner's bringing her in here to put her up for sale."

"She must be pretty big, then. Is Sam's boat man enough to tow her, do you think?"

"We'll have the flood under us," her friend said. "It'll be only a matter of keeping her straight. Sam got the orders from the office; take his boat down there and tow her in. I don't think he knows much about her."

"Doesn't care much, either."

"No. I suppose not."

Jean cleaned her brushes and put on a jersey. They walked down through the shipyard full of boats hauled out and boats laid up to where the launch was moored beside the jetty.

They inspected the aged launch and her equipment with distaste. "We'll want a better warp than this to tow the yacht with," said Jean. "How big is she, anyway?"

"I dunno," Deborah replied, eyeing a mass of warps upon the pier. "Shall we take this one?"

"God, it's all over tar," said Jean. "I don't suppose Sam's got a clean one."

"I don't suppose he has."

"Oh, all right," said Jean. "He might at least have pumped the launch out for us. Bet you a bob the motor doesn't start."

She tried the starter and the motor fired into life with a noise totally disproportionate to its performance. "Well, it goes, but it's got the whooping cough—just listen to it. All right, cast off the bow warp. All gone aft."

They turned the launch and headed away down the river, threading in and out among the hundreds of moored yachts, past Luke's Yard, past Hamble, past Warsash and what was once *H.M.S. Tormentor,* heading out towards the Solent. As they came near the Spit buoy they looked for anything that might have come from America, but all they saw was a salt-stained little fishing boat with black topsides and a painted mast, anchored.

"There's only that thing," said Jean Porter. "I shouldn't think that's it."

"Well, it's the only one there is," said Deborah. "We'd better go and see."

She turned the launch towards the anchored fishing boat. Roused by the sound of the engine, a man put his head out of the companion and looked at the approaching boat. Then he pulled himself up on deck. He was a youngish man in sail-cloth trousers that had once been white, wearing a very old blue pullover. Jean stared at him dumbfounded. "God," she said quietly to Deborah, "I know that chap. He—he's an old buddy. Used to be in the R.N.V.R."

Deborah brought the launch alongside and Jean caught the gunwale with a boat hook.

Deborah said, "Is this the boat that wants a tow in to the river?"

Donald said, "That's right. I've been sitting here since ten o'clock." And then he said,

"Hullo, Jean."

She said weakly, "Hullo, Donald." She could think of nothing apt to say, and so she asked, "Is this your boat?"

He nodded. "I bought her in Newfoundland. I gave up the insurance business—found I couldn't make the grade."

She said, "We heard something about a boat coming from America, but we thought she'd be bigger. Did you sail her over?"

He nodded.

"How many of you were there?" she enquired.

"Only me," he said. "I brought her over alone."

"Oh . . ." Behind her, Deborah Curtis said quietly, "He-Man stuff," with admiration in her voice.

Donald flushed a little, and said, "No, just out of money." There was an awkward pause.

Jean said at last, "We've come to tow you in." She busied herself with the warp. "Will you take the end of this, sir? I'm afraid it's a bit dirty."

A slow smile spread across his face. "All right, madam."

She was embarrassed and passed the warp up to him in silence. The girls watched him from the launch as he made it fast, and began to get in anchor chain. Deborah asked, "How long are you stopping here?"

"I don't know. A week or two, perhaps."

She said, "I'll tow you to a berth out on the posts, if that's all right."

The anchor came up and the girls put the launch ahead; the warp tightened and the *Mary* swung around behind them as they headed into the river. They could now talk confidentially, and Deborah said, "Why on earth did you want to go and call him 'sir'? We aren't in the Navy now."

Jean said quietly, "I don't know—it was silly to do that. I used to call him 'sir' in the old days."

"I thought you said he was a buddy."

Jean stared resolutely up the river, avoiding the interested glance of her companion. "He was once."

"Well, I wouldn't start calling him 'sir' again, or you'll be giving him ideas."

"I wouldn't mind."

"Probably beat you," said Deborah. "You want to watch out with these ocean racing types. They're tough."

In half an hour they came up to the mooring posts. They towed the *Mary* alongside one while Donald made his bow warp fast; then they took out his stern warp to another. Finally they laid the motor boat alongside. Jean asked, "May we come aboard and have a look at her, Donald?"

"Of course," he said. "But she's in the hell of a mess."

They climbed on board, and he began to show them round. Jean asked, "Did you come all the way in her single-handed, then? Without anybody to help you at all?"

He nodded. "Twenty-four days to the West of Ireland, to Galway. It wasn't bad, except that I got a bit short of sleep towards the end. I spent three days there and then sailed her round to Falmouth, and went up to London to find a decent yacht agent to see about selling her. I saw Scott and Harper. They said I'd better bring her here."

The girl smiled slowly, thinking of Donald as he had appeared to her in the Savoy, shabby and ill at ease. "Bit of a change from the insurance office, isn't it?"

He glanced at her in her sea kit, the wind blowing a wisp of hair across her face as it always had at Portland. This was the girl that had attracted him so greatly at Weymouth, not the shatteringly soignée one that he had met at the Savoy. "Bit of a change yourself," he replied. "I thought you'd packed up on all this sort of thing and gone to live like a lady."

She laughed. "I got fed up with living like a lady."

"I got a bit browned off with living like a gentleman," he said. "Pity we've got such low tastes."

He took off one of the hatch planks for them, and a strong smell of old, stale fish was wafted up around them. They looked down, wondering, into the hold. "She wants de-fishing a bit," said Deborah. "What are all the rocks doing down there?"

"Rocks? That's the ballast."

"Hasn't she got any other ballast—any iron keel, or anything?"

He shook his head. "That's the way she is."

"A bit crude, isn't it?"

"Maybe. It's good enough for crossing the Atlantic."

Jean said, "Sam Little knows where he can get pig iron for ballast, real iron in proper pigs. He says there's thirty-five tons of it in Southampton."

Donald looked at her; he saw the soft line of her neck as it passed below her jersey, that he remembered so well. He recalled his wandering thoughts. "I'd want about five tons, I should think. It'd be better to chuck out the rocks and get iron ballast into her before I try to sell her, wouldn't it?"

"I should think so," she said. "You're going to sell her at once, are you?"

"If I can." He hesitated. "I say, would you like a cup of tea? I've only got tinned milk."

He took them down into the cuddy and they sat on the bunk. The rest of the little space was filled with cooking gear and sails and coils of rope. There was barely room in it for the three of them at all. He made tea for them, using his one mug and the top of a Thermos flask and a chipped plastic toothmug, and he gave them cigarettes. Presently he asked, "How much do you think I'll get for her?"

Deborah said, "You mean selling her just so—just like she is? You'll have to clean her up a bit."

"I can't do very much to her," he said. "I'll have to get some cash in pretty soon. I'm just about broke."

"Too bad." Deborah was silent for a minute. "People will probably pay something for the fact that she's sailed the Atlantic," she said thoughtfully. "That should put about two hundred on the price. I should think she'd fetch five or six hundred pounds, wouldn't she?"

Jean said, "Oh, I should think so. You could make a nice yacht out of her, you know. That fish hold must be over fifteen feet long, and it's wide too."

"About twelve feet," said Donald.

"You could get some nice accommodation into that," she said. "Tell me, Donald, is the hull all right?"

"Sound as a bell," he said. "She's only fifteen years old."

"I wouldn't let her go for less than six hundred," said Deborah. "She'll be bought by somebody who'll do her up and sell her for two thousand."

Donald said, "If I could get six hundred pounds for her I'd be doing all right." He turned to Jean. "Tell me, what are you doing down here anyway? I thought you'd be in Northampton."

She said, "I'm living in a thing called *Joybelle*." He smiled. "Don't laugh—it really is her name. Her owner thinks it's a lovely name. We brought her back from Guernsey." She began to tell him all about the *Joybelle* and their voyage back from Cherbourg, and she was unreasonably pleased to hear him say quietly, at one stage of her account, "Good show." She told him what she had been doing while she had been living in her at the Hamble river for the last two months. "She's pretty nearly finished now," she said. "You must come and have a look at her tomorrow. She really is quite nice, if you like cabin cruisers."

Deborah said, "The darned things always make me sick." She got up. "I'll have to beat it and take Sam's boat back, or he'll be creating hell."

They all went on shore together to find a dinghy to lend Donald, who had none of his own; Deborah left them, and Jean took Donald to the shipyard and fixed him up with a small pram of Mr. Clough's on loan. And then he said, "What does one do about food here? Does the Bugle run a dinner?"

She nodded, "It's quite good. I have a meal there sometimes."

He glanced at her. "Have one tonight with me?"

She said, "I'd love to, Donald."

She left him to change into clean clothes. When she met him again, she was wearing a white blouse and blue linen slacks. They had a drink and dined together, talking eagerly. Deborah Curtis appeared once in the background, grinned, wagged her head at Jean, and went away.

Over the coffee after dinner, Jean said, "You know, Donald, you oughtn't to sell the *Mary* as she is. It wouldn't cost too much to build accommodation into her, and put in a second-hand engine. There was a chap up at Bursledon doing that to a Cornish lugger last month. He reckoned he was going to spend four hundred pounds on her. I don't believe you'd have to spend any more on the *Mary*, and then you could sell her as a yacht."

"For fifteen hundred?"

"Probably for more. Honestly, Donald—boats are going for the most fantastic prices. You wouldn't believe it."

He shook his head. "I'll have to let her go. I haven't got four hundred pounds in the wide world. I couldn't raise a hundred."

She was about to say something impulsively but thought better of it. Her money had already made one breach between them, and she didn't want another. Instead, she said, "I don't suppose you'd have to pay the bills before you got the money in for selling her."

He smiled at her in wonder. "I believe this business is right up your alley," he said curiously. "You seem to know an awful lot about it. You didn't learn that in the Navy."

"No. But you learn about buying and selling things at home, and if you're keen on boats it's just the same." Throughout her childhood she had listened to her father's business gossip with his friends, so that buying and selling came to her as natural ideas. Living at Hamble upon the *Joybelle* for two months had turned those natural ideas into the yachting channel. She was interested in the business of selling boats, as well as in reconditioning and sailing them. She was her father's daughter.

Mr. Porter recognised that two days later, when she turned up at his office in Northampton before going home to see her mother. "I'm only up here for one night," she said. "Daddy, I'd have come up anyway about this time to see you and Mummy, but what I've really come for this time is to ask you for some money. I want six hundred pounds to go into a sort of partnership over a boat."

He hedged instinctively. "What sort of boat?"

She told him all about it, about Donald Wolfe and his insurance job, about their meeting in Portland, about his single-handed crossing of the Atlantic. As she talked he watched her and reflected, "This is it." In the end she said, "It's a good bet, Daddy—honestly it is. I shan't lose the money. What I thought was, if we made a partnership or a small Company, or something, so that Donald could put in his boat worth six hundred as she stands, and I put in six hundred pounds in cash, we'd be even then, and we could split whatever we can sell her for after she's all dolled up."

He grunted, smiling a little. "Is that the only sort of partnership you've got in mind?"

"I don't know, Daddy. I do like him—awfully." And then

she said, "He'd never ask me or anybody else to marry him unless he'd got a bit of money, and he might make some this way. It's a terribly good market, Daddy. Honestly."

He said, "I've heard some cockeyed reasons for going into business in my time, but never one like that."

"It's a cockeyed world," the girl answered. "You've made a darned sight too much money, Daddy—that's my trouble. No decent man will look at me. It doesn't give a girl a chance."

He grinned. "If I hadn't, I wouldn't have six hundred pounds to give you."

"If you hadn't," she retorted, "I wouldn't need it."

Jean went back to Hamble early next morning, over the protestations of her mother. She got there early in the afternoon. From the deck of the *Joybelle*, she could see Donald busy painting something on the deck of the *Mary*. She went down into her cabin and changed into her working clothes, took her paint pot and a brush, and rowed off in the dinghy. Coming alongside the *Mary*, she said a little shyly, "I came to see if I could lend a hand. My job's practically finished on the *Joybelle*."

"Sure," he said, "if you like painting. I was doing this hatch, and then there's the inside of the bulwarks to be done, all round."

She climbed on board with her paint pot and her brush, and looked about her. "What are you going to do about the decks, Donald?" Beneath her feet the deck was rough and worn, and coming up in splinters here and there.

"I'll have to leave those," he replied. "One can't do everything."

"They're sound enough, aren't they?" she said. "I should think they ought to be planed smooth and canvassed."

His mind visualised the clean sweep of white painted deck that would result. "She'd look all right if that was done," he agreed. "Still, she'll sell all right as she is."

She filled her paint pot from the can. "Where shall I start?"

They worked on together for an hour in the afternoon sunlight, talking about his voyage home in the *Mary*, about cheap boats in Newfoundland, and about her trip home from the Channel Islands in the *Joybelle*. Presently they stopped for a short rest, and sat upon the rail together smoking cigarettes, held in paint-stained fingers, studying the work that still had to be done.

At last Jean said, "Donald, I was thinking about her. It seems an awful shame to sell her like she is—just chucking away money. I'm out of a job now. The *Joybelle*'s pretty well finished. Tony Clough's coming down for a week-end in her on Saturday. If I don't find something else to do down here, I suppose I'll have to go home. I was wondering if you'd let me come and give a hand with this."

"Of course," he said. "The more the merrier. But I shall have to sell her soon."

The girl stared over to the Warsash shore, avoiding his eyes. "I was wondering if you'd like to make a partnership of it," she said. "You'd get six or seven hundred for her now, but if we could doll her up properly she might fetch three times that."

He was silent, and she went on apprehensively, "I was thinking; if you put her into a partnership between us, and I put in cash to the same value as your boat, to make things even, we might both do all right on the deal."

There was a long, anxious pause. "It's terribly nice of you to think of it that way," he said at last. "I haven't got any money, as you know. But a partnership would have to be on even terms, and she's not worth anything like six or seven hundred as she stands. A chap in the Bugle offered me three hundred for her yesterday. I think that's more like it."

"You mean you wouldn't take more than three hundred cash from me if we went into partnership on her?" the girl asked.

"That's right."

"What about you bringing her across the Atlantic? That's

worth something, on your side. Three hundred's much too little for her."

He grinned. "I'll give you another hundred for the Atlantic. Four hundred pounds she's worth, and four hundred from you. That's my last word."

She smiled with relief. "Well, that suits me. It means we'll have to do a lot more work on her ourselves, and that means living down here all the rest of the summer."

"I thought you were going to do shorthand typing."

"Well, think again. I found I wasn't very good at it."

He glanced at her. "If you really want to do that with your money, Jean," he said quietly, it'd suit me fine. I've got nothing—as you know. I don't know what I'm going to do. I've tried insurance, and I found I couldn't make a go of it. I bought this boat on impulse, more or less, because I thought that I might make a hundred pounds or so on her. If I make a bit more through this partnership with you, it might mean I could go out again and buy another one in Trinidad or somewhere, and make a bit more. It seems a pretty crazy way to try and make a living, but I'd rather go on this way while it lasts than go back to the City."

She picked up an end of the cod line from the deck and began to splice it back upon itself. "I'm in the same boat, in a way," she said. "I know I haven't got to work, but that isn't the point. Maybe if there hadn't been a war and I hadn't gone into the Navy, I might have been happy to live at home, not doing much but go to dances and to parties, and take the dog out for a run. Or I might have been happy enough in an office doing shorthand typing, if I'd started young enough. But as things have turned out, I *did* spend three years in the Navy doing a real job, and now I can't just settle down at home, and take the dog out for a run. I've got to find something to do. And this messing about with boats—well, it's the only kind of job I know. It's what I like doing. That's why this partnership would suit me, Donald. Now the *Joybelle's* finished, I'd like to come and work on the *Mary*, and see if we can't make a decent yacht of her."

He said thoughtfully, "She's iron fastened, of course."

"I don't believe the average buyer cares a thing about the fastenings," she said. "All they think about is the paintwork and the appearance and the finish in the saloon. We'll have to find a decent cabinet maker. And whether the motor will start easily."

He glanced at her, sitting beside him, interested and immersed in the problem of the vessel. He smiled. "Partnership it is," he said. "But since it's between friends, we'd better have an agreement." She laughed. "We'll have to go and find a nice solicitor."

He thought for a minute. "Porter and Wolfe."

"No," she said quietly. "Wolfe and Porter."

"We'd better go over to the Bugle for a mug of beer to clinch the deal," he said. "It's open now."

They found Deborah Curtis in the bar of the Bugle with a young man who had just bought an oil well, and they all dined at his expense to celebrate it. He had bought an old naval motor gunboat hull without engines, intending to fit it up as a houseboat and live in it. His first chore had been to try to eliminate a strong smell of petrol before starting up a Primus stove. In the course of his investigations, he discovered that he had bought three hundred and eighty gallons of petrol with the hull, forgotten by the Navy and left in the starboard tank. At that time of stringent petrol rationing, that was a Godsend, and he paid for dinner in the exuberance of the discovery.

In the ladies' cloakroom after dinner, Jean said to Deborah, "I'm going into partnership with Donald."

"You needn't be so mealy mouthed about it," said her friend.

"I mean, really in partnership, as a matter of business. I'm putting in a bit of money and he's putting in his boat, and we're going to see if we can't make something decent out of her. We're going to make it a proper firm, with a solicitor's agreement and everything; Wolfe and Porter."

Deborah stared at her. "Is that what you're doing with him?" And she began laughing.

Jean tossed her head. "There's no need to go on like that," she said indignantly. "It's just an ordinary business deal."

"Says you."

Jean and Donald took their partnership very seriously, however; the only people in Hamble who did so. They went into Southampton next day and had a deed drawn up by a solicitor. When it was finished, Jean took it and showed it to Deborah Curtis with its big red seal and signatures, as proof that Wolfe and Porter was a firm of substance. Her friend said, "Just like marriage lines, dear, isn't it? Makes it all quite regular."

"More than you've got, anyway," said Jean.

She moved out of the *Joybelle* and took a bed and a sitting room in the village, ordered a ream of business notepaper with the name of the firm printed on it in big black letters, and sent to Northampton for her portable typewriter. In Hamble, Wolfe and Porter let it be known that they were prepared to undertake all kinds of yachting business.

Curiously enough, business began to come their way. Almost immediately, they got their first enquiry from one of the shipyards: Would they go and fetch a ten-tonner bought by a client and now lying at Brightlingsea on the East coast?

"Three days' job," said Donald. He hesitated. "There's just one thing," he said. "It really needs two people, and it means at least three nights away from here. I don't know what you think about that end of it."

Jean said, "Well, it's part of the firm's business, after all. It's all okay with me, so long as you don't tell Mummy."

They travelled to London next day in their seagoing clothes laden with untidy bundles of blankets and food. The last time Jean had been in London, she remembered, she had stayed at the Savoy, and everything had been too precious for words, and she had lost Donald as a result. Now, she rode quickly through by taxi from terminus to terminus, dressed in her old serge trousers and wearing an oilskin, carrying two loaves of bread wrapped up in newspaper and a string bag with a cabbage on top of some potatoes and onions and a few tins, but she was with Donald. She hardly glanced at the Savoy Hotel as they passed by it in the taxi.

They got to Brightlingsea in the evening, and found the boatmen and were rowed out to the yacht. They soon discovered that the water and petrol tanks were dry, and that the mainsail was at the sailmaker's. Her accommodation consisted of a forecastle and a saloon. There had been a curtain once between them and the curtain rod was still there.

"Going to be a bit matey tonight," Jean said laughing.

Donald said, "I say, would you rather sleep on shore?"

"Lord, no. We want to get off early as we can, don't we? We can fix up something."

They were determined to sail for Hamble first thing in the morning, and they worked on till dark fuelling and watering the yacht, carrying the heavy mainsail down from the sailmaker's shop half a mile away, and bending it on the boom. They set to cook supper then, at half past ten, almost too tired to eat it. By the time they had finished and washed up, it was close on midnight. They were so sleepy by that time that privacy for their undressing seemed a matter easy of solution; they just tucked a blanket over the curtain rod and went ahead. When it fell down at a critical moment they just laughed and tucked it up again. Ten minutes later both of them were sound asleep, Jean in the saloon and Donald in the forecastle.

Getting up in the morning presented them with a problem or two, which they surmounted without any undue familiarity, but they were both rather thoughtful as they sailed across the estuary of the Thames, both very conscious that there were two more nights to go before they reached the Hamble. Navigating through the sandbanks of the estuary was a job which kept both fully occupied till they were round the North Foreland, but presently a foul tide and headwind made it useless to plug on. They went to Dover harbour and anchored for the night at about five o'clock.

That evening they had supper on shore together in a cheap café, and went to the pictures to see Judy Garland. They sat in the warm darkness in very close proximity for three hours. When they came out the moon was bright. They walked down to the harbour, each a little nervous, and got into the dinghy and rowed out to the yacht.

That evening, things were very difficult for them. They were both wide awake for one thing, not in the least sleepy; and very much aware of each other. Jean brewed a couple of mugs of cocoa and they made themselves a little meal of bread and cheese and jam. Then they were ready for bed. The blanket curtain, made secure this time, was hardly adequate for privacy with their alert perceptions. It was impossible for one partner in Wolfe and Porter to be unaware of everything the other partner was doing behind the curtain, and the partners were very much aware of each other. To cover their embarrassment, they talked, which only accentuated the sense of intimacy. When finally they got under their blankets and put out the lights, they were thoroughly exasperated with themselves, with each other, and with the conventions that prevented a more natural arrangement of their lives.

Donald Wolfe lay awake that night nearly until dawn listening to the small movements of the girl as she lay in her blankets barely three feet away from him. He was very well aware that she was lying awake too. It was obvious to him that things were coming swiftly to a crisis between them, and he welcomed that with one part of his mind. He wanted nothing better than to take her in his arms and tell her what he really thought about her. On the other hand, he knew very well that everybody in the small society in which they moved at Hamble expected them to marry, and that the more cynical of their acquaintances were already saying that Donald Wolfe was doing very well for himself, marrying that girl. He was realist enough himself to see some truth in that. If he were to marry Jean Porter with hardly a penny in his pocket, he would indeed be doing very well for himself. No, love between himself and Jean would have to wait until he had, at any rate, a little money in the bank and a chance of making a bit more, if he were to retain any of his self respect. He lay awake and irritable, listening to her movements in her blankets, only three feet away.

Jean lay awake for much the same reason, and with the same irritation. In all his dealings with her Donald had been scrupulously correct. She could have happily thrown her mug of cocoa at him that evening for his studied impersonality. She rather wished she had. It might have precipitated something between them. She knew that he was lying wide awake only three feet away from her and she had a very good idea what was causing it. She knew that all Deborah Curtis' friends were saying he was on a damn good thing. In her mind, she cursed them heartily, with all the rude phrases she had picked up in the Navy. And yet, deep in her mind, she knew that he was right. Donald was what he was. She could not make him different with all her father's money, and she did not want to. When you got involved with a scrupulous man, it seemed, you had to be patient. All right; she would be patient, if it didn't go on too long.

She lay awake until dawn.

They got up stale, irritable and unrefreshed by their time in bed, and made sail after breakfast with about a hundred miles to go to Hamble. The wind was not directly ahead of them, but it was too much ahead to enable them to lie the course. They laid the yacht close hauled to the wind and stood off on a course that took them far out into the Channel. In the middle of the morning Donald said, "What would you think about it if we go right on, sail all night, and get it over with?

She warmed to the suggestion. She did not want another night alone with him like that, and she knew he felt about it as she did. She said, "I think that's a darned good idea, if it keeps fine. We'd better start keeping watches from now on."

He nodded. "I'll take twelve till four." That meant that he would have the hardest watch at night.

With that agreement, things immediately became easier between them. Each had the feeling that they had discussed their difficulty although they had not spoken of it; a slender, tenuous bond of sympathy now held them closer to each other, so that each had gained. At twelve o'clock Jean went below and cooked a meal and cut a vast quantity of sandwiches to last them through the night. Then she lay down with a blanket over her and slept till Donald came to shake her into wakefulness at ten minutes to four. It did not worry either of them very much now, when he touched her in her sleep.

They sailed all night in a light wind, picked up the Nab light at three in the morning, and stood into Spithead in the first light of dawn. They came to Hamble in time for a late breakfast. They handed the yacht over to the yard, took their fee, and then caught the bus into Southampton to go and look at a reconditioned marine engine that they thought of putting into the *Mary*. They paid eighty pounds for the engine, arranged for it to be delivered to Hamble, and went back to the Bugle for their supper.

There followed two months of happiness for them. They did not go away again together. They got several more orders for the delivery of yachts, but they tacitly arranged it so that one or the other of them went alone, or with some friend. With these interruptions excepted, they spent each day together working upon the *Mary*; working as industriously as a pair of beavers, as if their whole future depended on making a good job of the vessel, which indeed, it did. As the weeks went on, they came to know a good deal about each other, and it didn't put them off.

They took the *Mary* to the yard and had her put upon the slip, and had the sternpost drilled for the propeller shaft and had their second-hand engine installed. They gave her a couple of coats of antifouling paint and put her back into the water quickly, before the bill got any bigger. They were lucky to find an old cabinetmaker in the village who undertook to rebuild the interior of the vessel as a yacht, and they made several journeys to the towns round about to buy small parcels of fine woods, walnut, mahogany and cedar. With these and a good deal of resin-bonded plywood the old man got to work under their guidance, and the accommodation grew almost as they looked at it. They did all the painting and work on deck themselves, working long hours in the sunlight in the quiet serenity of the river.

Tony Clough had taken possession of the *Joybelle* by that time, and he came down to the yacht most week-ends to live in her as she was tied up very safely in the Hamble river. He showed very little inclination to go to sea again. He used to come and see them on Sundays as they worked in the *Mary*, motoring down the river in his smart dinghy. He would stand looking round at all they had done since he had been there last, giving them the benefit of his own views on the design of yachts. "Coming along fine," he would say thoughtfully. "Going to be a proper little yacht by the time you've done with her. I'm glad you've given her a cocktail cabinet; kind of makes it homely, don't it? I think you want to make room for a second head, though. Women, they don't like the same as men; not really, they don't."

In the end, Tony Clough proved to be the instrument of their deliverance. He telegraphed them one day to ring him up at Northampton. "I'm bringing a chap down for the week-end, as he wants to buy a boat," he said. "Keen as anything on sailing, he is, and his boy too. They don't want no motor yacht. I thought maybe the *Mary* would suit them. When the boy heard she'd sailed the Atlantic, he was nuts about her. His Dad says he can't talk of nothing else. Oh, aye—they've got the money."

He brought Mr. Seddon and his son along on Saturday afternoon, and Wolfe and Porter welcomed them on board. The interior of the *Mary* was not quite finished, but the top-sides and the deck were bright with new paint and varnish; the sun shone; and the motor started from stone cold immediately the button was pressed. The Seddons, father and son, stayed with them for two hours. The boy lingered over the dog-eared exercise book that had been the log of the *Mary* on her Atlantic crossing.

"That goes with her, of course," said Donald casually, with all the art of salesmanship.

The boy turned to his father, glowing. "Daddy, Mr. Wolfe says he'll let us have the logbook if we buy her. We could have it bound!"

They took the Seddons out for a short sail in the Solent the next day; by Sunday evening the ship was sold, for sixteen hundred pounds. Wolfe and Porter sat exhausted on the gunwale in the evening sunlight, watching the retreating dinghy. Three or four days' work to finish off the ship lay ahead of them. Next week-end they would hand her over and collect the balance of the purchase price.

"Sixteen hundred pounds," said Jean thoughtfully. "Eight hundred for you and eight hundred for me. Not bad going, when you come to think of it. Especially if you consider all the fun we've had."

He glanced at her, at the soft line of her neck as it entered her summer flannel, legacy of her Wren days. He forced his mind back to their conversation from quite irrelevant matters. "What are you going to do with yours?" he asked.

"I don't know. I suppose the original four hundred should go back to Daddy. What'll you do with yours?"

He said, "I think I shall go back to Newfoundland, or else to Trinidad, and try to do it again. But there's one thing that I'd like to do first."

She felt the crisis rising hot and strong between them. "What's that, Donald?"

"Marry you," he said.

She smiled. "Just like that?"

"Just like that," he said. "Tomorrow, if it could be fixed that way. If not, well, the day after."

A dinghy, sailing, passed close behind them with a little whisper in the water and the wind. Jean said, "It's a bit public here. We'd better go below and talk about it." So they went down into the unfinished saloon, and there they came together, and did very little talking for a time.

At last she said, "Did eight hundred pounds make all this difference to us, Donald?"

He nodded, laughing down into her face. "All of it."

She laughed up at him, secure in his arms. "What would have happened if we hadn't made it?"

"I don't know," he said. "We'd probably have done something pretty naughty, pretty soon."

She sighed happily. "I suppose we'll have to go home now for you to meet Daddy and Mummy, and tell them that you've got sufficient money to keep me in the style I'm accustomed to. That's the phrase, isn't it?"

He grinned down at her. "That's right. That's my story, and I'm sticking to it. The style you're accustomed to, and have been all those years. Gumboots and dirty clothes, and Primus stoves, and rough food, and salt water. Not the Savoy Hotel."

She stood thoughtful for a moment with his arms around her. "Not the Savoy Hotel," she said quietly. "I do like the

Savoy, Donald, but I couldn't spend my life there. Not now. I suppose that's what the war has done to me. Gumboots and Primus stoves and rough food and salt water. You mustn't expect that Mummy will ever understand. I think Daddy might, perhaps."

"We'll tell your mother that we're going out to Trinidad for our honeymoon," he said. "That sounds all right. We needn't say we're going looking for another cut price wreck."

She smiled. "All of the things we might have done," she said thoughtfully. "You might have had a good job in the City and done well, and had a nice home in the suburbs, and a settled life. I might have married somebody with lots of money in Northampton and had a Rolls Royce and a couple of hunters and lived like a lady. All that we've chucked away, because we neither of us could give up the sea. And so we're starting off together like a pair of ruddy fools, looking for old hulks to dish them up and sell them at a profit. We'll never get sensible, settled people to understand."

"Sorry?" he asked gently.

"No," she said. "I'd never trade this life for the Savoy."

Other Nevil Shute hardcovers
available from The Paper Tiger:

Landfall
Lonely Road
Marazan
Ruined City
Slide Rule
The Mysterious Aviator
Vinland the Good
What Happened to the Corbetts

Also now available:

Nevil Shute: A Biography by Julian Smith

The Paper Tiger, Inc.
335 Jefferson Avenue
Cresskill, NJ 07626
(201) 567-5620
www.papertig.com